Happy Reading
J. Von Scurter

UNPREDICTABLE

Would you like to know when future Lady Jenniviere's Quill books are released?

Visit: www.LadyJennivieresQuill.com

More stories from Lady Jenniviere's Quill

Tiffy's Terrible Top Hat

Tales of Spook

Alien Mission

Treasure Hunt

Costumes

Never Ending Bad Day

Get Well Before It Gets You

Unpredictable

COMING SOON

Stuffed

Skeleton Guy

Holiday Strike

Grimely

Unpredictable

Copyright 2015 by JENNIFER VON SCURLOCK

All rights reserved. Lady Jenniviere thanks you for not reproducing, scanning or distributing any part of this book without written permission.

PUBLISHED BY: Gold Hat Publishing

Original Art Work by Aprilily

Cover copyright © 2015 Gold Hat Publishing

ISBN PRINT 978-1-941723-15-9

ISBN DIGTAL 978-1-941723-16-6

This is a work of fiction. Names, characters, places, brands, media, and incidents are either the product of the author's imagination or are used fictitiously. The author acknowledges the trademarked status and trademark owners of any product referenced in this work of fiction, which have been used without permission. The publication or use of these trademarks is not authorized, associated with, or sponsored by the trademark owner.

For Mom... Your unconditional love gives my imagination wings, gives my ideas power and your confidence lights the path to a journey uniquely my own. Happy Mothers Day.

About the author: Lady Jenniviere's Story
Nelson and the Magic Ink-Well

Lady Jenniviere was like any other girl, until one day while tending her rose garden; she came upon an injured bird a cedar wax wing with a broken wing. Speaking quietly to reassure the frightened creature, Lady Jenniviere wrapped him in the folds of her gown and carried the little bird inside where, using tape and popsicle sticks, she set his broken wing. The bird was immediately grateful and thanked her for her kindness. He said his name was Nelson and asked if she'd mind if he hung around her palace while he recovered. Lady Jenniviere was delighted and the two became fast friends. Nelson enjoyed stories and asked Lady Jenniviere to read to him in her spare time. In the evenings, Lady Jenniviere sat in front of the fireplace with an old book in hand while her husband, Lord Mark of Tanglewood, their three dogs, Zoie, Mazi and Jordan, their parrot, Story, and Nelson gathered around to listen. On special occasions, Lady Jenniviere made up tales of epic heroes, spooky villains and mystical lands. These stories were Nelson's favorite. When his wing healed, he took Lady Jenniviere on a faraway hike up a tall mountain to a secret cave no human had ever seen. Inside the cave, he showed her a magic ink well, hidden away for centuries. He gave her the ink well as a gift for her kindness and hospitality. When they returned to the castle, Nelson pulled out a tail feather and instructed her to dip the quill into the ancient ink well. Amazingly, a story sprang to life and began writing itself upon the blank papers on her antique desk. Lady Jenniviere loved the story and thanked Nelson for his gift before he flew back to the forest on two healthy wings.

Soon, other birds heard of Lady Jenniviere's magic inkwell and brought her their tail feathers. Every quill revealed a different story—some scary, some happy and some just plain strange. Eventually, Lady Jenniviere had enough stories to begin sharing them with her friends. Books were bound and soon people everywhere were reading the tales of Lady Jenniviere's Quill.

Table of Contents

Fighting The Rules 1

Something Is Missing 17

Darkness Forever 24

A Dark Day 30

Another Mystery 64

Lady Jenniviere's Note 1

Smushy 66

An Expert's Opinion 70

Skeleton Mold 82

Liquid 84

Press Attacks 88

Cast Away Critters 96

Random Consequences 99

The Lake 109

Weird Effects 113

Slavery 121

The Blasted Rosenberg 126

Oranges 134

Off 138

A Wish 146

Don't Blow It 152

Saturday 155

Lady Jenniviere's Thoughts 160

Lady Jenniviere's Note

Best wishes, my avid little readers. I've got a strange story for you today, a strange story indeed. Dare I say, the strangest story I've ever heard. This odd tale found its way to me exactly one week ago while I was taking a peaceful nap in a friend's hammock. I do love a good nap. Anyway, a blue jay tapped me on the shoulder, handed me its tail feather and bid me adieu. Quickly, I disentangled myself from the hammock's thick web and hurried home to dip the quill into my magical ink. What unfolded kept me in suspense until the very end. Since this story is so exciting, I won't delay another moment.

Happy reading,

Lady Jenniviere

Fighting The Rules

Suzie Bing stomps one chubby, stinky foot in protest. "I hate rules. In fact, I absolutely abhor them. I never get to do anything I want. Why can't everyone just do what they want? Rules are just a way for adults to make kids miserable. Their lives are no fun so they want to make sure we don't have fun either."

"That could be, or perhaps the rules are in place to keep sassy thirteen-year-old girls from acting like sassy thirteen-year-olds," Ryder offers.

To Suzie, rules are only in place to make her young life miserable. As a bratty thirteen-year-old girl, she rarely gets her way. However, her older, respectful, well-behaved sister, Ryder, gets everything. This fact of life makes Suzie resentful. Nothing in her world is fair—or so she thinks. Being the baby of the family stinks. Never being listened to stinks. Ryder's life is much cooler than hers: her curfew is later, her friends are more interesting and the Bings impose way fewer rules on her. To sum things up, Ryder has the life. The world revolves around Ryder, while Suzie Bing has to sit back and watch.

Suzie trudges into her family's tiny wooden shack battling huge mosquitoes the entire way. They live in Florida. Not the good part of Florida with the beautiful sandy coast, vividly blue sea and lush wildlife; Swampville, Florida is the bad inland part where the town receives the humidity from the ocean and the bugs from the forests, but none of the perks. As if missing out on the good part of Florida wasn't the worst part of Suzie's life, her folks aren't the brightest bulbs on the Christmas tree, either. Mr. and Mrs. Bing are more like the bulbs that constantly short out, causing the whole tree to go dark during the middle of Christmas dinner. Her parents do what they can for a living, but permanent employment isn't their claim to fame. Working steadily isn't their forte. They dream of self-employment, the opportunity to run things themselves without having a boss hovering over them, but they don't have the self-discipline required. Every venture they begin just ends with a new pile of junk in the garage and dashed dreams.

The place they call home is a tattered hovel with mounds of "treasures," that no one else wants, and they are strewn everywhere throughout the tiny house. Suzie looks around at the place in disgust. Her parents horde things—

mainly cats. The foul air is pungent with the thick aroma of cat urine. Suzie plugs her nostrils, trying to avoid gagging. It takes about five minutes to adjust to the smell. She waits one minute and then unplugs her left nostril, then another two minutes before releasing her grasp on the right nostril. Three minutes later, she can breathe without her stomach roiling. Wading through the piles of trash and cat fur, Suzie makes her way through the living room, down the hall into the room she shares with Ryder.

The room is divided into two distinct halves. A clear demarcation line runs down the center. This line is not so much an actual line drawn on the floor, but more of a figurative line reflecting the sisters' differing personalities and views on personal hygiene. Ryder's side is immaculate, neatly decorated with golden awards, certificates and trophies from school. For some reason, no one can explain, Ryder's side smells like fresh oranges, the floor shines and there is not a cat hair or speck of dust in sight. Suzie's side is the exact opposite. Her side looks like the rest of the house—messy. Dirt and cat hair cover the dull floor leaving an ever-present smell of cat lingering in the air. It's tear-provoking, to say the least.

Angrily, Suzie scoots a sleeping black cat named Boo from the middle of the unmade bed and plops dramatically down. "I get an invitation to Taylor Ming's birthday party—the most important party of the year—and I can't go because we can't afford a gift. Can you believe that?" Boo gazes at Suzie with a look that reads either commiseration or tummy troubles from an upcoming fur ball. "I know. Mom rattled on about the importance of etiquette, that it is bad manners to arrive with empty hands. She thinks that if I show up without a gift, Taylor won't want me there."

Tired of listening to Suzie's whining, Boo hisses and runs off, hoping to find better company like a nice chewy mouse or chatty fox.

Suzie tries to seize the cat by the tail as the kitten flees her bed. She misses by merely an inch and says as Boo wanders away, "Thanks for being on my side, buddy. I know you agree that rules are stupid. We are better off without them. Really, when you think about it, they are just another way to hold us down."

Suzie looks down at her party invitation and sighs. Every girl in school is looking forward to Taylor's birthday extravaganza. Rumors about grandiose activities pervaded the school house's proverbial water-cooler for months.

Some said Taylor's mom actually hired One Direction to perform their best hits at the party. A boy from class said horseback riding was a given and a chocolate fountain was on its way in the mail. Taylor Ming is the rich kid in school. It never fails, every school has one. These rich kids are easy to spot. They are usually the trendy kid with the cool shoes, the shiny hair and the dad driving the convertible. Taylor's parents give her everything: private riding lessons, a working doll house in the back yard with running water and air conditioning that is bigger than the Bings' entire house. Taylor even wears couture. Suzie's not sure what couture is, but she is certain if Taylor has it, it must be good. Taylor has great personal style and the coolest toys in town. Everyone wants to be invited to that party. When Suzie finally received her invitation, she nearly fainted with excitement. Taylor invited her—the poor girl with the uncool wardrobe, frizzy hair and a dad who drives a car with a roof? Suzie finally earned a spot in the popular crowd. It was about time! This is a huge honor and now her parents are trying to wreck her social standing by forbidding her attendance to the shindig of the year. Taylor has so much stuff, she wouldn't even notice if Suzie didn't give her a gift. Right? Besides, the invitation didn't mention every attendee needs to arrive with present in-hand.

Leaning against her headboard, Suzie daydreams about chocolate fountains and being called onstage to sing with Harry Styles. Ryder taps on the door, interrupting her thoughts. "Mind if I come in?"

"It's your room, too. You can do whatever you want."

As Ryder passes into her side of the bedroom, she takes a deep breath then exhales slowly, as if smelling the first blooms of spring. The fresh air is a welcomed relief from the rest of the house. Sitting gently on the edge of her perfectly made bed, Ryder says, "I'm sorry you can't go to that party. I know it was important to you."

Suzie doesn't reply, but turns her back on her older sister. "I don't feel like talking about it!"

Ryder sighs patiently, hands folded in her lap. She smiles with the radiance of a meditating monk. Ryder never gets upset; it's simply not her style. Suzie considers her sister's even temper her most irritating trait.

Ryder says, "There will be other parties. You're going to attend gala events. Parties like those in fairy tales. I am sure of it."

Suzie grimaces, rolls her eyes and thinks Ryder's optimism is certainly her most irritating trait.

"I'm only trying to help. It's like that saying, 'Change what you can, accept what you can't and be smart enough to know the difference'."

"Well, I refuse to accept this. I've worked hard to get into the popular crowd. And there won't be other parties. At least, not like this one. This is one for the history books. You just watch."

"Can I give you some big-sister advice?"

"No, you're only one year older. That doesn't make you a wise old sage. It makes you a fourteen-year-old with bad acne and skinny legs. Besides, the only advice you can give me is how to wear deodorant since you hit puberty and now have smelly pits," Suzie huffs, still facing the wall." By the way, do you know how irritating it is when you quote self-help gurus? I think it might top the list of your most irritating traits."

"Why are you always so mean? I never mention your smelly feet."

"Why do you always have to be so perfect?" Suzie asks, finally turning to face Ryder. "I get tired of being compared to you all the time. 'Ryder does her homework',

'Ryder doesn't talk back' and 'Ryder is so skinny'. Do you have any idea how exhausting it is always taking second place to you?"

"You'll lose your baby fat soon, Suzie, don't worry."

"You're missing my point. I didn't say I was worried. I don't care that I'm fat. I like being fat. The rules say I should be thin and I hate the rules so that's why I like being fat. So there. Besides, fat is back, or haven't you heard?"

"I had no idea," Ryder says, looking down at her lean torso. "But I do have an idea so you can go to that party, if it's so important to you."

"You have lots of ideas. I don't care."

"No, you will like this idea. I think I know how you can bring a gift to Taylor's party."

Suzie's fudgy-colored eyes light up. "You're going to help me steal something?" she asks, chubby face wide with excitement. For the first time in their lives, Suzie thinks Ryder might actually want to help her. It's about time they are finally on the same page.

"What? No, of course not. How could you think such a terrible thing?" Suzie, we may be poor, but we aren't thieves. We earn what we need. I can't believe you!"

Suzie looks at her older sister with rage. Ryder doesn't have a bad bone in her skinny body. She even looks like an angel with long blonde hair, light green eyes and perfect teeth. Sometimes, Suzie wonders if her parents didn't adopt Ryder and keep it a secret. Their parents are chubby like she is with dark hair, dark eyes and crooked, winged-out teeth. "Well, Einstein, if we aren't going to steal the gift and we don't have money to buy the gift, what exactly are you proposing?"

"Let's make Taylor something. It will have more meaning this way. Everyone values the thought behind handmade gifts. What types of things does she like?"

"She likes expensive things you buy from fancy stores. Making her something is the dumbest idea in the world. Can you imagine how stupid I would look walking into the party with a homemade craft-project gift? Come on, Ryder. This is Taylor Ming we're talking about. If it isn't couture, she isn't impressed."

"First, do you know what couture is?"

"Not exactly. I'm guessing it has something to do with being very expensive and I think it has to look funny, too. Picture an expensive clown outfit with super-tall high heels, that's couture.

"Well, that's not the technical definition, but you kind of hit the nail on the head. That's a surprisingly accurate description. Anyway, you want to go to that party, right?"

"Yeah, you can't even imagine how bad I want to go to that party. If I could go, it would ensure my place among the seventh-grade 'it' crowd. I would go into eighth grade next year as a cool kid. Junior high would be a success. High school would bring dates to the prom, a ticket on the cheerleading squad and a lifetime of admiration after that. Seriously, Ryder, this party means the Big Time in terms of popularity. If I'm not popular, what's the point?"

"Suzie, there are more important things in life than being popular. You have to like who you are and never compromise your principles. Character is like a tree and reputation like a shadow. The shadow is what we think of it; the tree is the real thing. We'll only be in school a short time compared to the rest of our lives and it's better to be a good person than a cool teenager."

Sticking out her tongue, Suzie rolls her dark eyes. "Who cares about life after school? I can't imagine what adulthood is like and right now I don't need to, but I do need to figure out how best to survive junior high! And, by the way, I don't know who the tree quote is from, but I know you read it somewhere and didn't come up with it on your own."

"I'm serious. Don't stress out about being popular. I assure you, it's not the most important thing in the world. You may think that now, but you'll see. Anyway," Ryder continues, "the tree quote is from the esteemed Mr. Abraham Lincoln."

"Yeah, popularity isn't important to you. You are like the biggest nerd at Swampville Junior High School. Every day you eat lunch alone. No one likes you because you say weird stuff about the importance of being a good person and having personal principles. You act more like an adult than a kid. Not only did you just randomly quote Honest Abe, you knew who you were quoting. That makes you weird. I'm already at a disadvantage just by being your sister. I have to work extra hard at acting cool to compensate for your weirdness. Do you know how much work that is? No, of course you don't. And, while we're on the subject, I do worry about my principles. Like, for instance, one of my principles is that I hate rules. Rules say I should bring a gift. Well, I've decided I'm going to that party and I'm not bringing a gift. What are they going to do? Kick me out because I showed up empty-handed?"

Ryder watches her sister jump off the bed, plant her chubby arms firmly on her hips and nod with satisfaction. Suzie is proud of her decision and feels like she's recently uncovered one of life's deep, dark mysteries. She stomps around her side of the cluttered room for a few minutes, trying to decide what to do next. For Suzie, this is a huge, life-altering decision. It's going against the grain, a rebel decision, telling the rules of life, "I am not impressed. You no longer have the power to influence what path I choose. From now on, I am a path finder! Everyone else can have their rules, I am choosing fun."

Shaking her head, Ryder mutters, "Oh boy, we're in for trouble now!"

"I'm going to tell Mom and Dad my decision," Suzie says, shuffling out of the room in haste. Both parents are sitting on the lopsided front porch in old wicker chairs long faded from too many years in the Florida sun. They sip iced tea and chew on sunflower seeds while watching the clouds roll past overhead. "I have an announcement," Suzie declares.

"Not now, Suzie-Q," Mr. Bing says. "We're relaxin'. You can't interrupt us during our relaxin' time."

"You and Mom are always relaxing. This is important. I need to tell you something."

Mrs. Bing spits a sunflower seed hull into an empty milk jug before slowly shifting her gaze from the clouds to her youngest daughter. "Tell us quick, baby, before Daddy can't relax no more."

"I've decided I'm going to Taylor's party without a gift. I don't need one. Rules are silly and I have to go to that party. It's imperative for my social life."

"Where are you learnin' all them big words, Suzie-Q?" her father asks. "Imperative means important, don't it?"

"Yes, Daddy. It's important for my social life. Taylor's party will make or break me."

"To be honest," Mr. Bing says, looking toward his wife, "I don't care one way or the other."

"Fine, baby, go to that party. But if you feel bad, it's on you, not us. Don't come home crying, saying I didn't tell you so beforehand."

"Yes, ma'am."

Suzie beams with pride. She's pulled off a real coup. "Take that, rules," she screams to the sky with her fists striking the air." Instantly, the clouds thicken and the sky darkens. The gorgeous day turns chilly. An angry northern wind howls. Every leaf blows wildly in the wind, the trees bend with the force of an onrushing storm. Huge raindrops pelt the barren ground.

Mr. and Mrs. Bing rush for cover, anxious to avoid the frigid storm. They slam through the front door, shivering inside the living room. Together they peer out from a bare window in the front room, wondering where the storm came from while they wait for their senses to adjust to the smelly cat odor. "Well, so much for my relaxin' time," Mr. Bing says, wandering to the kitchen for a cup of coffee to warm his suddenly chilled bones.

"I think you shook your fist at the wrong cloud, baby," Mrs. Bing jokes. "Nothin' was happening till then. Then, like the wrath of Zeus, this big ol' storm comes blowing through our front yard."

Suzie stands by the dusty window, petting a mangy-looking cat while watching the storm. Tornado sirens blare down the road from the volunteer fire station.

Ryder runs into the living room with her premade tornado kit in-hand. "Listen up, Bing family. First, I need everyone to stay calm; next, I need you to follow me into the bathroom." Mr. Bing abandons his cup of coffee while

Mrs. Bing attempts to herd the clowder of cats to safety in the bathroom.

Like a freight train roaring beside the house, the wind howls outside. The Bings and a slew of flea-ridden felines huddle together in the shallow old bathtub with Ryder's mattress over the top of the tub for added protection. Tree limbs, pine cones and other assorted debris pelt the roof. The wind yowls, shaking the walls of the worn-down shanty. The Bings hold on to one another tightly, hoping for the best while preparing for the worst.

Something Is Missing

The Bing family stands in the front yard, staring at the damage from the tornado. Amazingly, the old house still stands, but randomly placed piles of debris dot the ground. Trees are down, power poles are cracked in half and the neighbor's travel trailer is nowhere in sight. There's no rainbow at the end of this storm; only darkness. Despite the day's early hour, the sky is pitch-black. It feels like the sun packed its bags and moved to the other end of the universe, leaving the residents of Swampville to fend for themselves.

Ryder begins clearing away fallen tree limbs, broken clay pots and the disheveled lawn art the Bings have picked up over years of hyper-diligent yard-sale shopping. Plastic gnomes are scattered over the walking path to the unattached garage, old tires are hanging from the rusty metal supports of the clothes line, broken yard equipment is strewn along the back storage shed and their life-sized cowboy mailbox is on the tin roof!

Mr. Bing wanders across the street to talk to his neighbor about the missing RV while everyone else studies the damage outside. No one is hurt, the cats survived and nary is a leak found inside. Although the electricity is still off, no one complains. Surviving a tornado is a gift and no one wants to gripe about the ravenous mosquitos eating away at their legs or mention the high humidity making them feel like they're collecting trash inside an over-sized sauna. Even Suzie respects the day now, secretly grateful for escaping the storm with life and ears intact.

Ryder hums as she cleans. Suzie watches her older sister, laughing callously to herself. She has no intention of lifting a finger to help with the renovations. Tidiness isn't her forte. While swatting away pests and strolling through the yard trying to look busy, a stroke of genius hits her. She can tell Taylor that her birthday gift blew away in the storm! The idea is brilliant. While envisioning what present suddenly went missing in the storm, she bumps into Ryder holding a trowel in one hand and a giant-sized pinwheel in the other. "Hey, watch it!" Suzie screams. "You nearly stabbed me with that trowel."

"It would take a wooden stake or, better yet, a silver bullet to kill you," Ryder jokes.

Suzie doesn't laugh. "That's not funny. I'm not a vampire."

"Yeah, as bad as your feet stink you might be a werewolf," Ryder says. Thinking her joke is hilarious, she walks away, laughing at the top of her lungs. Suzie looks toward the sky and notices how brightly the stars are shining. Normally, the sky isn't dark enough to see the stars clearly. There's something about the sky that isn't right. Almost like something is missing. Mrs. Bing interrupts her thoughts. Her chubby face is lit up from the citronella candle burning in a small tin she's carrying. "I'm pooped," she says, wiping away a thick layer of smelly sweat from her brow. Large circles of perspiration stain the giant armpits of the gray undershirt she wears. It isn't a pretty sight. No woman her size should wear only an undershirt. A real shirt is required at the minimum and probably a girdle at the maximum. Not that a girdle could do much to contain the five hundred pounds of blubbery belly that is barely disguised behind the thin layer of gray cotton. "What are you thinking about, baby?" Mrs. Bing asks, head tilted toward the ebony sky.

"What's missing in this picture," Suzie replies.

Mrs. Bing shrugs her thick shoulders. "Don't know. Don't care," she says. "I'm gonna take a cold bath and wait for your daddy to cook us some dinner."

Suzie watches her mother waddle into the cramped hovel before turning her attention back to the sky. Astronomy has always fascinated her—stars, moons, planets and the entire solar system with its black holes, galaxies and possibility of life in outer space.

"Whatcha thinking about?" Ryder asks, done with her clean-up mission at last.

"I want to be an astronaut when I grow up. I'm going to travel to the moon, to Jupiter, to Mars…even to planets we haven't yet discovered."

"I thought you weren't concerned with adulthood? Anyway, have you heard the news that two astronauts may have discovered a new planet on their latest space mission?"

"No, really?" Suzie asks, fascinated.

"Yeah, it's real far away, but they call it planet Zoot. I've even heard rumors that it may contain life, although the powers that be swear the life isn't intelligent."

"I heard about a UFO landing in San Francisco a few months ago. A flying saucer touched down on the Golden Gate Bridge and then just disappeared into thin air. If that alien was from planet Zoot, then they are way more advanced than we are."

Mrs. Bing yells from inside the house, "Girls, it's dinner time. Don't you keep us waitin' now, ya hear."

"We'd better go before Mama gets mad," Ryder says. "But hey, I want you to know that you can be an astronaut when you grow up if you want to."

"Yeah, I know. That's why I said I want to be one."

"I just mean that you don't have to settle because we aren't rich or because Mom and Dad are, well, not the sharpest knives in the drawer. I'm going to college and you can too."

"What do you want to do?" Suzie asks.

"I want to be a writer."

"Supper time," Mr. Bing hollers from the porch. The girls have done it now. Mr. Bing is angry. He rapidly taps his foot, making his point that time is ticking while Suzie and Ryder stand around chit-chatting about the future.

Inside, Mr. and Mrs. Bing pile onto the sofa before pulling up their old rusty TV trays as makeshift individual tables. Tonight, Mr. Bing went all out. On the corner of each tray sits a citronella candle, perfect for keeping the mosquitoes at bay. To Mrs. Bing, the soft flickering of the candlelight provides a romantic ambiance. She flashes a smile in her husband's direction. He's a real charmer when he wants to be. The girls plop down in front of the TV with bowls of cold pork and beans.

In the Bing house, meals are served in the living room in front of the television—except for Thanksgiving and Halloween dinner, when Mrs. Bing insists they celebrate the holidays in proper, civilized style. On these two occasions a year, the accumulated junk is cleared from a small office desk that poses as their dining room table. Ryder scrubs away the cat hair, uses a paint scraper to remove the dried, caked-on spills from the previous holiday and Suzie sets up a crate in the corner of the dining room that Mrs. Bing uses as a TV stand. It wouldn't be a proper holiday meal without television, but watching their standard big screen would be disrespectful to ancient pilgrims and long-lost goblins, so they haul in the mini TV set instead. This TV is reserved exclusively for Suzie the other 363 days a year and sets atop the big screen. Mr. Bing dedicated it to his youngest daughter to resolve the conflict of her obsession with The Weather Channel. For some odd, unknown reason, Suzie prefers to stay updated on weather-related traffic delays for all forty-eight contiguous states. The rest of the family was tired of her stealing the remote to check the weather on the eights of every hour. When Mr.

Bing found the old, tiny TV during one of his many garage-sale hunts, he happily brought it home. Suzie was happy. The Bings were happy and luckily Suzie doesn't mind sharing her screen on the holidays. It's her way of adding a little holiday cheer.

Sadly, it isn't Thanksgiving or Halloween so the Bings settle into their usual places. Mr. and Mrs. Bing sit side by side on the old worn-out couch eating their pork and beans from their rusty TV trays while Suzie and Ryder balance their bowls on their laps. Any other night, the roaring din of situation comedies would combine with weather updates on the eights to prevent conversation. Yet tonight, with no electricity, the Bing's are unsure what to do. Ryder smiles contently, Suzie glares at no one in particular, the parents stare at the blank TV, and the horde of cat's meow loudly, trying to fill the uncomfortable silence.

Finally, the night wears on and one by one the Bings grow tired of the quiet and retire to bed. Each hopes the sun will come out tomorrow.

But the next day, the sun doesn't rise.

Darkness Forever

Ding. Ding. Ding. Ryder slams down her fist atop her alarm clock, silencing the loud buzzing siren. Rubbing sleep from her eyes, she stretches and stares out the window at complete darkness. Yawning, she picks up the alarm clock, staring at the red numbers: 8:00 a.m. She places the clock back on the night table and checks her watch: 8:00 a.m. Curious, Ryder turns on the bedside lamp, ushering light into the black room. Thick snoring invades her ears from her parents' room down the hall. She wants to wake them to discuss the oddity of the morning, but knows the house rules well. No one is to disturb their parents unless it's an absolute emergency. She glances at Suzie, still sleeping peacefully in her bed across the room. Two cats are nestled in between her feet, licking her stinky toes.

Ryder pulls aside the Little Mermaid sheet that serves as a curtain and peers out. The sky is dark as a moonless night. Silence fills the outdoors. No birds sing. No rooster crows. No mosquitoes buzz. Is it morning? Why do the clocks say it's dawn when the sky disagrees?

Anxious for answers, Ryder taps Suzie on the shoulder. "Hey, I need you to wake up. Something strange is happening. Suzie, listen to me." She shakes her sister's tubby body. Finally, Suzie stirs, slowly opening her brown eyes while yawning. The disgusting scent of morning breath assaults Ryder's nostrils.

"What do you want?" Suzie snaps.

"First, I want you to brush your teeth."

Suzie lets out a huge breath, blowing right in her angelic sister's face. "If you didn't wake me up, then you wouldn't smell my stinky breath." She looks around the dark room. "What time is it? It's still dark out."

"That's what I'm worried about. I think it's eight o'clock in the morning, but the sun isn't up yet."

"Is it raining?" Suzie asks between stretches and yawns.

"No. No rain. No signs of rain."

Suzie sits up in bed, rubbing crusty eyelids. She checks her watch. It reads 8:05. "Let's consult The Weather Channel. We can get an update in three minutes. If The Weather Channel doesn't know, then all hope is lost. The Weather Channel knows all!"

I seriously don't understand your odd fixation with [W]eather Channel. You act like it is magic."

Suzie doesn't reply and Ryder figures in this case, checking The Weather Channel isn't a bad idea so Ryder follows her sister into the living room, flipping on the small-screen television. Despite the family's poor financial status, they have a fifty-inch television set. Being poor doesn't stop the Bings from enjoying their favorite TV shows in style. Although Ryder would happily trade the big screen for more dinner options, no one else shares her culinary concerns. Pork and beans every night is rough on her digestion system. And equally rough on her poor classmates who constantly endure her gassy outbursts. It may be part of the reason she doesn't have many friends. Okay, doesn't have any friends.

Suzie knows The Weather Channel's number by heart and punches it into the remote for her mini television screen. "Emergency" flashes in red over and over again. Then the words: THIS IS NOT A TEST. THIS IS AN EMERGENCY. THE SUN IS DEAD. DARKNESS FOREVER.

Ryder immediately shuts off the little television, not wanting to alarm her little sister. It's too late. Suzie is already scared. Real scared. "How did the sun die? Why did it die? Will a new sun take its place or is The Weather Channel right and we're doomed to darkness forever?" There's nothing comforting to say. No one ever expected the sun to die suddenly, without warning. This phenomenon wasn't expected for eons. No sun is a scary concept. It is always there every morning, rising dutifully from the east like a beacon of hope for the entire world. Without the sun, what will happen to Earth?

The sisters stare at the dark television sets for several minutes, thinking about the consequences of life without a sun. Finally, Suzie flips on a light. The brightness helps calm their startled nerves until Mrs. Bing groggily stumbles into the living room still wearing her stained gray undershirt. "What are you two doing up at this hour? How many times have we told you not to watch TV in the middle of the night?"

"Mama, it's morning," Ryder explains.

"Sure it is and I'm the Easter bunny. Very cute. Now go back to bed before your dad hears you."

"No, I'm not kidding. This is not a joke. It's almost nine." Before Ryder can finish, sirens from the fire station begin blaring a warning alarm. This siren is unfamiliar. It's not the tornado warning or the fire truck sirens. This is more sinister. More unforgiving, with its shrill piercing scream.

"Oh, don't tell me it's another awful tornado." Mrs. Bing sighs, preparing for another night in the shallow bathtub."

"No, listen, Mama. It's worse than that. I have terrible news. You're going to want to sit down for this," Suzie says.

Mrs. Bing backs up toward the couch when she feels the edge against her knees, she plops down. A solid black cat named Maxwell and a long-haired black and white cat named Pooter narrowly escape being crushed.

"Oh, Mama, the sun is dead!"

Mrs. Bing doesn't blink or move a muscle. Even her fat rolls stop jiggling. "The sun died?"

Ryder flips the small television back on. From the dented screen, the word "Emergency" flashes in bold red letters. The same message scrolls across the middle of the screen: THIS IS NOT A TEST. THIS IS AN EMERGENCY. THE SUN IS DEAD. DARKNESS FOREVER.

Outside, screams pierce the air. The neighbors are awake. They realize this Saturday morning is unlike any before. This morning is dark. Scary. Chilly. Mrs. Bing hurries to the porch as fast as her tree-trunk-sized legs will carry her. She joins in the screaming. No one is thinking. No one is trying to figure this out. It's chaos. Pure, maddening panic.

Mr. Bing stomps down the hall, angry for the disturbance. "What's the meaning of all this noise? It sounds like we're havin' a parade outside. Who is paradin' down the street in the middle of the night?" he demands.

Suzie is too freaked out to explain. She simply points to the open front door and ushers him out. The covey of cats add their screeching to the already deafening noise. Ryder puts her hands to her ears, trying to shut out the fearful screaming. This is the worst day ever. She's had bad days before, but none like this. There was always light at the end of the tunnel. Now there will never be light again.

A Dark Day

Mrs. Bing slams the lopsided front door shut as she re-enters the messy, smelly living room. Her face is sour with confusion and grief. She looks like a fat, old wizard who is too lost in her own thoughts to know what to do next. Her mouth hangs open, revealing a handful of crooked, rotten teeth. Mr. Bing puts his arm around her neck, hoping to calm her.

"I'd say it's time for a Bing family meetin'. We've got to think fast to survive this disaster. Where can we go? How will we get there? What can we do? Ryder, you're the smartest one in our group, so what do you think?"

Ryder swallows and shakes her head, cursing her bad luck at ending up with parents who expect her, at fourteen years old, to solve the crisis of the world ending. Nevertheless, what they do next is on her shoulders. "There's no place to go. The sun is dead, which means there's no light anywhere on Earth. We can't do anything. This is beyond our control," she says.

Suzie doesn't look convinced. Her sister may be the brains of the family, but Suzie has a few ideas she'd like to share. Without waiting for anyone to ask her opinion, she breaks into a rapid speech. "I think we need to turn on the news and see what they suggest. Everyone looks like they are leaving town. If we leave, we'll use what's left of our gas sitting in traffic. I know you need water in emergencies. I suppose water is of upmost importance now, too. Let's try to stay rational and think this through. The news will have scientists who know what's going on. Let's wait for them to explain why this is happening. Then we'll get our hands on as much water as possible and research our options rationally. The worst thing we can do is lose our heads and panic. Frantic inactivity won't help us survive."

  She speaks with such calm authority that her family listens. They like her plan. It makes sense. Ryder turns the television back on, searching for the news channel. Every cable station is off the air with a blank emergency green screen reading: WARNING. The local channels are fuzzy with black and white static zigzagging through the set. Ryder keeps flipping through the channels, hoping to find something helpful. Suzie crosses her fingers, praying her plan will work. Finally, two well-dressed reporters pop up on channel 102. With serious expressions planted on their well-made-up faces, they sit behind a huge desk discussing the possibilities of life on Earth with no sun. Their guests are four top scientists. The prognosis is grim, one of them says.

"What does that mean?" Mrs. Bing asks, scratching her sweaty armpits.

"It means we're all going to die," Ryder shouts. Suzie hushes her and turns up the volume on the TV.

Another scientist with a solar system necktie continues. "We can't say for certain what happened to the sun. It didn't explode as we all assumed it would billions of years from now. The truth is we don't know where it is or why this happened. We know our planet is still on its axis circling the non-existent or at least non-visible sun with the same gravitational pull as before. It's as if the sun is still present in our galaxy, but the light is gone. The Earth needs the sun's hot rays to survive. Without it, human life will surely parish quickly. The surface temperature of the Earth is already dropping."

"I knew it was colder in here," Mrs. Bing says, breaking everyone's concentration. Her family ignores the comment.

"The vegetation will die without the nutrients from the sun. Without proper vegetation to eat, mammals will starve. It's difficult to say at this point which scenario will occur first: humanity starving to death or freezing to death. The simple fact remains that we've never seen the rules of the solar system shift like this. The universe has a natural set of rules it's always followed since the beginning of time. To change them suddenly means the end of all we know and the beginning of the end altogether."

Ryder flips off the news. "That's not helping," she declares. Suddenly, she looks at Suzie. "This is what you get for thinking that rules don't matter and that you don't have to obey them. See, even the solar system has rules, the universe has rules, and you think you don't need rules?"

"Why are you yelling at me? Just because I hate rules doesn't mean it's my fault that the sun died."

"I know you didn't cause the sun to die, but I'm telling you that rules are important. Your big idea about not having to follow them is stupid. Even the universe has to follow them."

"But it didn't follow them. Today the sun didn't rise. The universe stopped following the rules. I guess even the sun was tired of conforming to the 'rules' all the time. What about free will? What about choosing our own destinies? Perhaps the sun got tired. Decided it needed a vacation.

Maybe wanted to spend some time with its sun family. That's possible."

"Yeah, it's possible. The sun has one simple task—shine brightly. That's it. Everything else in the universe will circle around it, and all it has to do is glow. Now it looks like the sun decided to make new rules and see what happens to us when it did. We're all going to die just because the sun didn't want to follow the rules!" Ryder screams.

Mr. and Mrs. Bing stare at their girls in amazement. They have no idea what this odd conversation is about. It seems a silly thing to argue over, given the extremity of the situation. Finally, Mr. Bing breaks in. "Ya'll are driving me crazy. I can't stand listenin' to this nonsense one more moment. I'm hungry. What do ya'll want for breakfast?"

His question doesn't sit well with his wife. "How can you think about food at a time like this? We're on the verge of extinction and you're worried about what we're going to eat for breakfast? How 'bout we try to figure out a plan? You know, some way of surviving the coming ice age? You been watching those shows about preppers on TV. Do any of them enjoy a nice leisurely breakfast then attempt to survive near-certain death? No. What we need is some planning. I bet this is what happened to the dinosaurs—a giant asteroid hit and it got dark and cold. Rather than work on a plan, the dinosaurs worried over what to eat for breakfast and now they are extinct."

Mr. Bing is at a loss for words. His stomach growls loudly. "See, I'm hungry. I can't get nothin' done on an empty stomach." With that, he marches into the kitchen and fires up the griddle for French toast. It may be the end of the world, but a guy's still got to eat.

The noise from the neighborhood is gone. Their street resembles a ghost town. Everyone on Skunk Lane left in a hurry. They took their pets, their pictures, their purses, locked up and headed to higher ground. Ryder grabs her jacket and walks outside. She studies the sky. There's something beautiful about its darkness, about the silence of emptiness. The stars shine brightly above. The moon glows in a half arc of light yellowy haze. According to the television scientists, the stars are distant suns, so they should shine with or without the Earth's sun. The moon, however, is a different story. They say the moon does not actually shine its own light, but reflects the light from the sun. So with no sunshine there will be no moonshine. Yet, nothing about the sky seems out of place.

A screech owl hollers in the distance behind the neighbor's barn, causing Ryder to nearly jump out of her skin. Suzie walks up behind her and chuckles. It may be a world-wide crisis, but it's still fun to watch the angelic one jump. Ryder smiles when she sees her sister and says, "I think it's kind of nice out here. I don't see what all the fuss is about."

"I'll tell you what all the fuss is about. It's nearly ten o'clock in the morning and it's pitch-black out here. This is a fine night, but it is a terrible day. The roosters aren't crowing, the paperboy isn't out slinging newspapers into people's shrubs, birds aren't singing, Mrs. Armstrong isn't mowing her yard and Old Mr. Gates isn't sitting on his front porch, waving to folks as they drive down the alleyway. This is not what a Saturday morning looks like. It's scary. It's the scariest thing I've ever seen." Suzie shivers and tears stream from her eyes.

"Hey, cheer up. You still have Taylor's birthday party this afternoon. That's going to be fun."

The phone rings in the kitchen. The Bings might be the only family left in the world without a cell phone. An old yellow phone with a long curly cord hangs on the kitchen wall. Its ring tone is loud and startles everyone with its shrill buzz. Mrs. Bing's muffled voice radiates outside. Suzie realizes she's talking to Taylor.

"That's for me! Hold on, I'm coming!" she screams, Grabbing the yellowy phone tightly then pressing it to her ear, Suzie screams, "Taylor, happy birthday!"

"Happy birthday? Are you kidding me? This is the worst day ever. It's completely wrecking my birthday. How dare the sun die on my thirteenth birthday! That is totally rude and thoughtless. I'm a teenager, hello? The sun should recognize that. Does the sun not realize who I am? Who my parents are? I'm writing a nasty letter about this."

"Who are you writing the letter to?" Suzie asks, confused. Surely, the sun isn't receiving mail at this time. If it left a forwarding address, it wouldn't be missing.

"To the president. He needs to know about this," Taylor declares. "I'm thirteen and having a bad day. It's an outrage!"

"I'm pretty sure the president knows the sun died today. I imagine the scientists briefed him first. Not to hurt your feelings, but I kind of think most thirteen-year-olds have bad days. As I understand it, it's a hormone thing."

Taylor doesn't reply; nevertheless, her rage radiates across the line. Like a smack from an invisible hand,

Taylor's anger reaches through the wire and whacks Suzie in the gut. Stunned, Suzie responds, "What do you want, Taylor?"

"I called because my parents canceled my party this afternoon. My thirteenth birthday party. Unbelievable. I've waited for this event for thirteen years. Now, I'm supposed to call everyone and tell them the horrible news. This is so unfair! I hate that this is happening to me. I'm like the most unlucky girl in the world!"

Suzie rolls her eyes. Taylor Ming is far from unlucky. She might be the luckiest girl in the world. Her family is rich. Taylor is healthy, smart and cute. She has an adorable Shih Tzu puppy named Mazi. What more could a girl want? Other than the sun to shine on her birthday, perhaps.

Taylor continues. "Well, since my party is ruined, you at least have to tell me what you got me. I'm asking everyone. It helps ease the pain of this terrible injustice. So, tell me, Suzie Bing—what amazing gift would you have given me today?"

"What did I get you? Um..."

Ryder rushes to her sister's side, shaking her head. "Don't lie," she whispers.

"Suzie, come on, tell me. I'm dying to know. You won't ruin the surprise. My birthday is totally ruined now anyway."

"I got you…"

Just as Suzie rattles into her story, Ryder steals the phone away, slamming it back on its hook attached to the kitchen wall. "I did that for your own good. Lying is a bad habit. No one likes liars. Taylor's birthday present isn't worth it."

Suzie's brown eyes open wide with alarm. "Who cares what I tell Taylor? They aren't having the party anyway. I can't let her think I didn't get her anything. I mean it, Ryder, I'm this close to getting into the cool crowd," Suzie says, putting her fingers only inches apart. "This means everything to me. I want to be in the 'it' crowd."

The Bings look at their daughters again, wondering what all the fuss is about. Mr. Bing is piling French toast a foot high on a wooden plate beside the stove. "How about we all settle down and eat some food? A full stomach always makes bad situations better."

*****

Many hours later, the night creatures finally give up waiting for morning and stop singing. Owls stop hooting, the crickets cease chirping and the croaking frogs fall silent. The firehouse's siren has also given up. Animals and people don't know whether to go to sleep or get up. Suzie sits on her bed reading *Teen Beat* magazine by the light of her desk lamp. The scornful look on her chubby face reveals her displeasure at the day's events. Had the sun risen, she'd be happily ingratiating herself in the cool crowd at Taylor's party. Since it didn't, she's stuck inside the rat trap house reading on a Saturday.

Ryder's Saturday plans aren't the least bit impacted. Her normal weekend routine includes a lot of down time for reading, writing and studying homework.

"I don't know why you're bothering with homework when we're in the middle of a disaster," Suzie says, looking up from her magazine. "Not having to do homework is the one good thing about the end of the world."

"The world isn't going to end. The scientists will develop a plan. They can probably make an artificial sun. If they can make artificial hearts, artificial legs, artificial sugar and fake cheese, how hard can it be to replicate the sun, anyway? Nothing bad will happen. In a few days, the sky lights will pop back on and we'll all feel silly for worrying about this. Besides, I can't let my homework slip. My GPA is nearly tied with Dobie McGill's. I'm one difficult test question away from being in second position."

"Oh no. The horror of second place," Suzie jokes. "Forget the fact the sun died, there's bigger news at stake — Ryder Bing might lose at something."

Their mother hears their laughter and wanders into their bedroom. Maybe their laughter will brighten her mood. Without the sun, she's completely unsure how to proceed with her normal daily routine of resume writing and word-search puzzling. If there's one thing Mrs. Bing can do well, it's write a resume. As an expert resume writer, she always gets the job. Her issue is keeping the job after she gets it. Early mornings, being on time and taking orders doesn't suit her particular skill set and employers find her errant behavior difficult to accept. Soon, she's back on the sofa, circling Help Wanted ads and writing more impressive resumes. Suzie certainly comes by her dislike of following rules naturally.

"Whatcha talkin' 'bout?" Mrs. Bings asks, hovering in the doorway of the girls' room.

"Nothing," Ryder and Suzie say.

"I'm gonna watch some more TV, if you want to watch it with me. Maybe they have better news to report now. Come on, keep Mama company for a while."

The family gathers around the giant television, listening to the same news report that aired earlier in the day. No one has any more insight to offer. Scientists continue to scratch their heads, completely baffled. The only updates available are the amount of people who called in sick for work, the number of people buying their dream car, booking flights for vacations they can't afford and the extravagant amounts being charged on credit cards for various toys. The entire world is suddenly no longer concerned with the future. All bets are off. It seems Ryder is the only person worrying about the consequences of her decisions. While psychologists interviewed on the news expected morale to be low, the opposite is proving true. Local reporters swarm the airports, interviewing families taking vacations, talking to people flying home to visit loved ones. The mood is upbeat and happy. Everyone seems pleased to finally have some time to do what they've always wanted to do in life. It seems the sun dying forced most people to actually begin living.

"Maybe we should go somewhere cool, too," Mrs. Bing suggests. "Why should those other families get to live it up and not us?"

"We don't got no money," Mr. Bing echoes, quickly dismissing the idea before even considering it.

"I want to go somewhere cool," Suzie whines. "If everyone else on the planet is doing something, why shouldn't we?"

"Because we can't afford it," Ryder, the ever-somber presence in the house, explains. "Besides, what would we do with Gus, Boo, Sassy Paws, Monster Man, Snicker, Snuffer, Mickey, Stir fry, Gizzer, Milo, Maxwell, Hokey, Pokey, Smarty Pants, Dexter, Winnie, Chester, Tuffy, Feather, Asphalt and Pooter? We can't abandon the cats!"

"What to do with the cats is the least of our worries," Mr. Bing says. "This discussion is closed."

"Not so fast, mister," Mrs. Bing says. "I want to go to the Mall of America. If all them people are chargin' up their credit cards with stuff they can't afford, I want to get me some stuff, too!"

"Where is the Mall of America?" Suzie asks. "I've never heard of it."

"It's in Minneapolis, Minnesota," Ryder calmly explains. "And even if it were only in Pensacola, we still couldn't go. We can't buy a bunch of stuff we can't afford. It's wrong. I can't miss school, Mom and Dad need to find new jobs. There's a lot going on right now, so we can't just up and leave."

"That's exactly what we're going to do. I'm calling my sister. She can watch Gus, Boo, Sassy Paws, Monster Man, Snicker, Snuffer, Mickey, Stir Fry, Gizzer, Milo, Maxwell, Hokey, Pokey, Smarty Pants, Dexter, Winnie, Chester, Tuffy, Feather, Asphalt and Pooter. Girls, go pack a bag of vacation stuff. We're going to the Mall of America!"

"I know the cats seem overly interested in your sister, but she gets awful nervous around them. You really think she'll take care of them while we are off vacationing in sunny Minneapolis?" Mr. Bing inquires.

"Just don't you worry about that. I'm sure sister Birdie will feed the cats. Now, you all need to get to packing."

Suzie rushes to her room, Mr. Bing reluctantly shuffles off to find suitcases while Mrs. Bing picks up Stir Fry and dances around the room, singing, "We're in the money." The white cat howls with her as she spins him around in the air.

Ryder asks, "Do you know anything about Minnesota or the Mall of America? I have no idea why you want to go there. You've never mentioned it before."

Mrs. Bing stops dancing. "I know it's on the ocean by California and that the mall is the biggest in the world. I have friends who say it's amazing!"

Ryder shakes her head. "No, Mama, wrong! It isn't on the ocean or near California. It's a metropolitan hub in the Midwest, located on the banks of the Minnesota River. In the summer, it's warm and humid. In the winter, snowy and cold. It's no California, Mom. Don't get me wrong, it's a fine city, but Minneapolis isn't the place to go if you're looking for ocean views and California weather."

Mrs. Bing's corpulent face scrunches into a nice flat pancake as she ponders Ryder's words. "Well, if it's on the Minnesota River we can at least go to the beach."

"No, Mama. Rivers don't have beaches."

"I don't care. I've decided Minneapolis is where I want to go. It's my dream vacation spot. We can shop until we drop; that will be fun. Come on, Ryder, you're fourteen years old. Teenagers love malls and this is the biggest in America. Now, get ready, young lady!" her mother orders.

*****

The Bings' Buick has other plans. Mr. Bing jiggles the key in the ignition, urging the old buggy to rev to life. Camilla, as the Bings call their beloved Buick is twenty years old. She's rusted everywhere except for a small patch on the roof, revealing that the car's original paint color was an ugly pea-green once upon a time, three of the four tires are bald and a mysterious bullet hole mars the driver's door. Finally, Camilla coughs, sputters and grinds to a start. Inside, the family waves goodbye to Aunt Birdie and their clowder of cats. What a relief to get away from the house, the yard filled with piles of junk left by yesterday's tornado, the house filled with piles of junk left by the family's unwillingness to clean and away from mountains of cat fur. The old Buick is no luxury, but she feels better than the inside of the house. Luckily, the heat actually works, which is a huge improvement over the house furnace. Amazingly, the little car gets them to the airport without overheating or breaking down along the highway. The airport's parking garages are packed with people rushing to get away from their boring lives and live a little before Earth freezes over.

Mr. Bing finds a spot for the car, drives over the yellow curb, scraping the bottom of the frame, and cuts the engine. "I'd reckon she's good for another hundred thousand miles," he jokes.

The Bings enter an international airport swarming with people. The crowd is so thick they have to carry their bags because there isn't foot room to pull them. The Bings stand in line for hours, waiting for a turn at the ticket counter. Eventually, they reach the head of the line. A lady in a blue uniform asks where they would like to go in a strict tone that screams, "I'm not happy about being here at work, while everyone else in the world boards a plane for vacation."

"What's wrong?" Ryder asks, feeling compassion for the woman behind the counter. As if her day isn't going poorly enough, that snug blue suit is doing nothing for her pale complexion and pudgy midsection.

"Really? That's a silly question. I'm working today while everyone else is getting out of town. I haven't seen the light of day in almost twenty hours. That's what's wrong, little girl."

"You don't have to be rude!" Mr. Bing says. "You chose to work today. If you want to go somewhere, you should print yourself off a ticket, pack a little carry-on, find a better-fitting outfit and fly away to your dream destination. What you shouldn't do is talk mean to my daughter."

The lady in blue doesn't appreciate Mr. Bing's wisdom and takes the opportunity to choose that moment to go on break. She smiles sweetly before placing a sign on the counter that reads "Lane Closed. Back in Ten." She walks away, humming to herself, looking for change to buy a bag of chips from the vending machine on the third floor.

"Well, now we're in a pickle. Why do you always have to open your big mouth and make a problem for the rest of us?" Mrs. Bing asks angrily.

"I was just sticking up for our kid. Why you gettin' mad at me?"

After 23 minutes, the lady returns, takes down her sign and asks, "Where to?"

"Minneapolis, Minnesota."

"Nope. Not an option. Got somewhere else you want to go? There are no more flights to Minnesota today. You can come back tomorrow or go somewhere else." The uniformed lady smiles. "Life's full of tough choices, isn't it?"

Mrs. Bing turns her head toward the crowd of people behind her packing every inch of the airport terminal. In disgust, she turns to face her family. "I don't want to return tomorrow! I want to leave today! I already made up my mind where I want to go and I won't have you tell me that I can't go there now!"

Blue suit says nothing, smiles, pops a wad of green chewing gum in her mouth and chomps loudly while the Bings decide what to do next. Finally, Mrs. Bing sighs and says, "What's left?"

Mrs. Uniform reads her computer screen. "Chicago, Illinois, Dallas, Texas, Columbus, Ohio, Denver, Colorado, Atlanta, Georgia, Costa Rica, Portland, Maine, Salt Lake City, Utah and Kansas City, Kansas."

Mrs. Bing scrunches up her nose, offended at the options. "I don't want to go to any of those places. They all sound terrible!"

"That's all I have left leaving today," the lady says, scratching her belly bloat and blowing a bubble with her minty gum.

"I like the idea of Salt Lake City," Suzie says. "Let's just pick a place and go. I don't care where. It's the journey that makes life fun anyway, not the destination."

Mrs. Bing shakes her head. "I don't know what the point of this is, anyway. It's not like we're going to see any of the landscape. Everything will be dark. And a mall is just a mall. I can go shopping right here in Swampville. Come on, let's go. This is a total waste of our time."

The family excuses themselves from the line and returns to the old Buick. "What time is it?" Ryder asks.

"It's nearly five in the afternoon," Mr. Bing says.

The parking garage is engulfed in darkness. Overhead fluorescents light up the individual parking spaces, but it's impossible to see beyond a few feet away. Staying awake is hard. With the darkness swirling around them, it feels like the middle of the night. Their bodies fight for sleep.

Mr. Bing sighs, then says, "I'm all tuckered out. Why don't we agree to do this vacation thing later? We can go home, maybe heat up a can of pork and beans, watch a little TV and get some sleep. The end of the world isn't today, so let's get some shut-eye and figure out what to do later. He makes a good point. At least as good a point as one would expect in the middle of a parking garage darkened by the death of the Sun after a day spent fighting crowds of people hoping to max out their credit cards before the world slowly freezes. If they can't go somewhere interesting, why not return home to the mess and the cats, eat some warm pork and beans, get some sleep and see what tomorrow brings? At this point, it's anyone's guess what will happen tomorrow. With the rules of the universe in flux, anything is a possibility.

They return home, release Aunt Birdie from cat duty and collapse onto the living room sofa. According to the news, panic is still high. Scientists, astrophysics and the White House are quickly working on remedies to save the Earth. Each expert interviewed has various solutions to the fix the problem; they vary greatly in severity. A gentleman by the name of Mr. Booth feels the solution is simple. Humans simply need more vitamin D to mimic the effects of the sun on the human body and the entire problem will be fixed. When asked how the other animals, vegetation and climate would be fixed by vitamin D, he has no real answers. Dr. Brown from the University of Oklahoma says she feels the only solution is to find another acceptable hospitable planet and quickly begin moving people in space ships. She is already in the process of working on spacesuits that humans can wear on Venus to shield themselves from the inferno-inspired environment. Her patent is still pending so she isn't willing to discuss the prototype of the Venetian spacesuit. If Venus isn't a possibility, she plans to consider planet Zoot next. Now that life was recently confirmed on the newly discovered planet, it might be a possibility. After all, that cute little boy from the Golden Gate Bridge proved that Zootlings might be open to sharing their planet with human beings. What cannot be known with certainty is if they would accept humans, pets and humanity's most prized masterpieces. Finally, the interviewer explains that Earth's sun is also the sun of Venus and Zoot. Dr. Brown says nothing but phones her lawyer to cancel the patent on her Venetian spacesuit and leaves the air rapidly. Following her dismal interview, another pseudoscientist explains that a giant cosmic space heater is the answer, though she readily admits she doesn't know how the space heater will foster the process of photosynthesis in plants or regulate the seasonal shifts. These types of interviews continue for hours. Not a single person has a plausible plan. Every possibility mentioned is wrought with holes and miscalculations. Apparently, no one ever considered the need to replace the sun should something happen to it. All of a sudden, it was a ridiculous notion that humans have lived on the planet for roughly

200,000 years without anyone implementing a back-up sun. Ironically, theatres hire understudies for the star parts in plays, but no one ever considered an understudy for the actual star of the universe.

Weary and confused, the Bings finally decide to call it a day. Is it a day if the sun doesn't shine? Well, to call it a twenty-four hour period, anyway. Mr. and Mrs. Bing had fallen asleep several times throughout the news programs. They found it difficult to stay awake with no lights anywhere outside. They weren't the only ones. The birds feel confused and tired, the animals are jet lagged and the night creatures don't know which cues to use. Is it the owls' time or the larks'?

While Ryder and Suzie trudge down the hall to their room, a sharp knock from the door catches their attention. Ryder glances at her watch. It is ten o'clock. Fearing the worst, she answers the door. To her surprise, a young woman dressed in a nice skirted suit stands on their dilapidated front porch. "Hi, I'm with channel nineteen. Yours is the only family that stayed in this section of Swampville. Would you mind if I interviewed you and your parents for a piece I'd like to run tomorrow on the morning show, *Wake up, Swampville*?"

Ryder stands at the door, baffled. Why would a reporter care about her family? They have to be the most boring people on the planet. Even on a dying planet. "Is Aunt Birdie back?" Mrs. Bing yells from the master bedroom.

"No, Mama, it's a reporter from channel nineteen. For some reason, she wants to do a story on us."

"Goodie, I haven't been on the TV since they interviewed me about that UFO I saw a couple of summers ago," Mrs. Bing says, rushing down the hall toward the front door.

"Mama, you know that wasn't a UFO. It was a lawn chair with a bunch of 'Happy Birthday' balloons attached," Ryder reminds her mother.

"I know you think that. But you can't prove it. That makes it an unidentified flying object. Or a U-F-O for short." Mrs. Bing smiles, proud of her powers of reason.

Mrs. Bing greets the reporter. "Hi there. I'm Beulah Bing. How nice you want to do a story on little ol' us. What can I tell you about my life?" she asks, face flushed with excitement. To Beulah, the Bings aren't boring people and she's glad someone finally recognizes the family's importance.

The young reporter looks her up and down for a moment, completely speechless. In Beulah Bing's hurry to introduce herself to the reporter, she neglected to find a robe. Standing in front of the reporter is Mrs. Bing in all her five-hundred-pound glory, wearing mix-matched shower shoes and a beach towel. Unfortunately her outfit leaves little to the imagination.

Ryder looks on, mortified. This is the single most embarrassing moment of her life. She pops her head around her mother's large frame, looking for a camera crew. The only way this could get any worse is if a camera crew is filming every second of this humiliating exchange. The last thing she needs is this video showing up on YouTube. Her low popularity would plunge to devastating new depths.

Suzie, however, doesn't mind her mother's crude attire and runs to the door to greet the reporter and to see if there is anything she can add to the interview. Perhaps the reporter needs the perspective of a thirteen-year-old girl. Mr. Bing is right behind her. It seems the entire family is more than willing to add their two cents to the problem at hand. Ryder, not wanting to be associated with this in any way, politely excuses herself and returns to her bedroom to hide in shame.

The rest of the Bing family isn't tired anymore. They spring to life like a fat pet parrot on pizza night. Inviting the nice reporter into the living room, Suzie turns the lamps back on and Mrs. Bing offers their company peach tea. "Come on in, honey," Mrs. Bing coos. "I'd be delighted to fetch you some tea or something a little stronger, like a cola."

"Oh no, ma'am, I couldn't," the reporter answers, looking around the hovel and at the hordes of trash scattered everywhere. She sneezes loudly four times in a row. Ryder hears the noise from her bedroom and prays this piece doesn't make the cut for Swampville's morning show.

"Well, before we start fillin' your head about us, tell us something about yourself," Mr. Bing says, clearly impressed by the young woman's poise. It's not every day someone fancy from the television shows up in their living room.

"My name is Wandy Vall. I'm technically still an intern at the TV station, but I'm hoping a big story could catapult my career and get me hired on full time after I graduate from college. Can you believe this day? What are your thoughts? Why did you stay? What are you most afraid of?"

"Wow, missy. That's a lot of questions," Mr. Bing says, trying to take in all her comments. "I don't know where to begin. You talk more than a mile a minute, young lady."

"I do," hollers Mrs. Bing from the crammed, dirty kitchen. "I know right where to begin. And I can believe this day. I've always been waitin' for something like this to happen one day. I've seen them prepper shows and I've always respected them people for havin' a plan when the bad stuff starts."

Mr. Bing eyes his wife suspiciously. "Oh, come on now, Beulah, you have not. You watch them shows and laugh."

"That's not true. Pay him no mind. I do watch them shows and think those folks are on to something," she retorts with more seriousness than a woman in a threadbare beach towel and flip-flops should feign. "I, myself, have always been a planner. Without a plan, you ain't going nowhere in life. That's what I always tell my girls. Ain't that right?"

Suzie shakes her head. She's never heard that line before in her life. Mrs. Bing is no planner. A hoarder, yes. A planner, no. Suzie can't stand her mother pandering to the reporter another second so she speaks up. "Mrs. Vall, I can't believe this day. It comes as a shock to all of us. When I woke up this morning and the sun wasn't up, I nearly had a fit."

"Were you frightened?" Wandy Vall asks.

"At first I was, but my big sister, Ryder, told me everything would be okay and Ryder is always right so I knew not to worry too much. I'm sure someone smart will figure this out. In fact, I want to be an astronaut when I grow up," she boasts, trying to say things that will make nice quotes for the show tomorrow.

Wandy Vall doesn't write down Suzie's words. Instead, she turns back to Mr. Bing and asks again, "Why did you stay in your um... home? Everyone else in the neighborhood is gone. They fled the area."

Mrs. Bing returns with peach tea, setting a huge jelly container down on the coffee table. The brown chunky liquid bubbles around a single used straw from a fast-food restaurant. Wandy Vall eyes the drink suspiciously. "Um, no thanks. I just had my teeth bleached and can't drink anything brown or anything chunky."

"What a shame," Suzie says politely before stealing the guest's drink for herself and sucking up a chunk of canned peach through the used straw. "Delicious!" she adds after a tiny burp.

Ignoring her daughter and hoping to reclaim the spotlight, Mrs. Bings says, "I wanted to go on vacation since I saw the airports full of people taking vacations of a lifetime on TV."

Her comment intrigues the reporter. "Why didn't you go?"

"Oh, we tried, but when we got to the airport, all the good places were already taken," she adds, nodding with a sad face.

"Good places? What does that mean?"
"They only had boring, Midwestern cities left. I mean, I'm not wasting my money on that, even if it is the last vacation of my life."

"Where were you headed?"

"Minnesota—the Mall of America."

"The Minnesota in the Midwest?" Wandy Vall asks.

"Yes."

"So you were going to use your savings to take this trip?"

"Well, no, not exactly. We was gonna charge it like all them other folks on TV. I figure it like this: we're all going up in a ball of smoke anyway, so chargin' it ain't hurtin' nobody." Suzie's mother sips her jar of tea.

The reporter detects a new story angle and decides to run with it. "Have you always felt this way or has your picture of right and wrong changed since this happened? Would you say all your ethics changed the minute the sun didn't rise this morning?"

Beulah Bing is uncomfortable with this line of questioning and looks like a deer caught in the headlights of a roaring semi-truck. "I, um—I, well—You're makin' it sound bad when it ain't bad at all. I mean, I deserve a fancy trip before I die, don't I?"

"Why would you deserve a trip you didn't earn?" Ms. Vall asks sincerely.

Ryder hears the reporter's question and rolls her eyes. This interview is going from bad to worse. Her family doesn't stand a chance; she has to intervene before her parents make fools of themselves.

Mrs. Bing continues. "Times have been hard. Work is scarce. Well, at least any work I want to do. Rules are difficult to define. Once the sun dies, does anyone really know what's right and wrong?"

"Yes, I think so. But it doesn't matter what I think. I'm not being interviewed. Tell me more about what you think," Wandy says.

Ryder arrives to save the day. "I think it's time for you to leave now. It's late and as you said, it's anyone's guess what will happen tomorrow. We don't have anything interesting to say about the sun's disappearance."

"No, but it is interesting to see how the locals are handling this situation. This has been quite helpful. You can watch your story tomorrow morning. I'm thinking of titling the piece, 'When the Rules Don't Apply to the Sun, They Shouldn't Apply to Me'."

"I think the rules still matter," Ryder defends. "Right and wrong still exist. As long as there is one human left on the planet, morality will endure."

"Very well said." Wandy Vall scribbles the statement down in her notebook. "It's good to see everyone hasn't lost their mind," she says out loud. "Of course, you can't lose what you never had," she murmurs under her breath. With that she thanks the Bings for their hospitality, then reminds them again their piece will air on channel 19 at six a.m.

Ryder slams the door shut angrily. She isn't angry with the reporter. She was only doing her job—her job is to find and report a story. Her mother, however, should have known better. "What if the kids at school see that interview?"

"I'm proud of your mama," Mr. Bing interjects. "She made some good statements. You ought to be proud of her, too."

"Suzie, do you still think the rules don't matter after all of this?" Ryder cries, hoping her sister at least has learned the lesson.

"Yep. They definitely don't matter. I agree with Mama. Stealing isn't hurting anyone when there's no one you're stealing from. It isn't stealing when you don't know who something belongs to."

Ryder groans. "Stealing is stealing and it's wrong no matter what. Just because you don't know who owns something, doesn't make it yours. By your logic, anyone can take the Buick from the grocery store parking lot as long as they don't know it belongs to us."

Mr. Bings laughs. "No one could get Camilla running and you know it."

Ryder stands with her mouth gaping like a fish out of water. Their logic is so convoluted that her brain is unable to follow the argument. Suddenly, her gray matter coils up tightly and takes a vacation of its own.

"What if you're hungry?" Suzie asks, trying to turn Ryder's statement into a philosophical discussion. "Is it all right to steal then?"

"I don't know. I'm tired. We aren't hungry. That's the point. We don't need a vacation. You don't need to lie to Taylor and pretend you got her a present when you didn't. This is the stuff I'm talking about."

Suzie and Mrs. Bing shrug their chubby shoulders. They aren't interested in an argument about morality on a sunless day or even a sunless night.

Everyone stomps off to bed, hoping to see the sun in the morning, but fully expecting another dark day ahead.

Another Mystery

The glorious sounds of birds chirping awaken Ryder. She's immediately filled with hope. If the birds are singing, is the sun shining? Crossing her fingers and slowly opening her eyes, she waits with anxiety. She looks around the room. It's lit! No lights in her room are on and it's bright! Jumping from bed, she rushes to the window, pulls back the curtains and admires the lovely day. Sitting on the horizon like a giant beacon of hope is the sun. It's alive and well! The sunlight illuminates the thick grass in the front yard, the chicken coop with its red roof, the rusty old Buick parked in the driveway. Everything looks better than she remembered. It's a gorgeous sight. The best she's ever seen. Without bothering to awaken Suzie, she runs through the house, opens the front door and dances under the perfectly clear sky. Warmth from the sun's rays heats her chilled skin. It's an amazing feeling. The Earth is warm again. All is right in the world.

When her lungs burn from running in circles around the front yard, she drops to the ground, gasping for breath. Monster Man and Pooter lie on her chest, enjoying the sunlight themselves. She pets the black and white kitties while blowing the remnants of a dandelion through the air. This is a perfect day.

Finally, she tires of being alone and wanders inside to wake her younger sister. Today is the ideal day for a picnic down by the lake at the edge of town. She and Suzie often ride their bikes down there and spend the afternoon by the water during hot summer days. It's not summer, but in honor of the sun's miraculous recovery, she decides a picnic is the only way to celebrate.

Her sleepy sister lies in bed, snoring powerfully under the covers. Only stringy, tangled strands of brown hair are visible atop her pillow. Ryder pulls the green quilt from Suzie's sleeping frame and screams in horror.

Smushy

Suzie is barely recognizable. Her body looks like a deflated pile of Jell-O loosely floating on the bed. Ryder is afraid to touch her little sister for fear that her finger will poke all the way through Suzie's skin to the bed itself. Unaware of Ryder's hovering frame, Suzie continues to snore. "Wake up, Suzie! Wake up, please!" Ryder begs.

Finally, Suzie's brown eyes pop open. A look of terror crosses her smushy face. "Something is wrong! I can't move my arms. I can't move my legs. What's happening to me?"

"Try to stay calm," Ryder whispers. "It's going to be all right. I'm going to get Dad. He'll know what to do. Just don't try to move, okay?" She fears her sister will roll right off the bed and shatter into tiny droplets of flesh and blood.

"Is this happening because the sun died?" Suzie asks, searching for an answer to her bizarre condition.

"No. The sun's up again. It's back. But don't worry about that right now. Stay still. I'm getting Dad." Ryder runs from their bedroom, leaving Suzie alone, mushy and afraid. Winnie jumps onto her stomach. His furry feet step lightly around her thin skin before he lies down. The image before her eyes is horrifying. The black cat looks as if he's sleeping right on top of the bed. He's no higher than an inch above the mattress. The weight of her body is gone. It's like she has no form left.

Mr. Bing rushes to his youngest daughter's side. He turns to the window and puts his hand over his mouth. Once he quells the urge to scream or hurl in revulsion, he turns back to Suzie. In all his years, he's never laid eyes on anything like this before. Tears stream from his eyes. He wants to hold Suzie's hand and tell her everything will be fine, but he's afraid to touch his own daughter. Her hand looks too weak to hold. Her body is nothing but a puddle of flabby form. He turns his attention to Ryder. "Is it possible for bones to disappear overnight?"

As soon as he utters the word 'bones', Ryder realizes that is exactly what Suzie is missing. Her bones are gone. Everything else is intact, but the strength of her skeleton vanished overnight. Suzie panics when she hears her bones are missing. She looks down at her diminished, missing frame and cries with fear and frustration. Immediately, she understands why her body feels like it's about to run off the bed—without bones, she has no control, no stability. Her support is gone! "Daddy, what are you going to do? Someone stole my bones! You have to find them and get my bones back!"

"Don't you worry, sweetie, I promise I'll find those dirty rotten bone thieves. And when I do, I won't rest, nor eat, till I get your bones back!"

Stunned, Ryder listens to the conversation. Unable to stop herself, she says, "What are you two talking about? There are no bone thieves. Someone didn't sneak in here during the night and steal Suzie's bones. Think about it—that makes no sense. Come on, people, we have to think rationally."

Suzie looks at her sister. "Okay, Mrs. Know-It-All, if someone didn't steal my bones, then where did they go?"

"Look, I admit I don't know what happened. I do know one thing: no one sneaked into the house and stole your bones. Just like last week when Mom couldn't find her favorite pair of sweatpants. For forty-five minutes the three of you stomped around the house trying to figure out who stole them. Mama called Aunt Birdie and accused her; Dad, you thought it was a government plot and Suzie, you concluded it was the work of gypsies. Turned out they were hanging on the clothes line. So we can spend the next few hours searching for possible bone thieves or we can call a doctor."

"A doctor?" Suzie says. When it's time to call the doctor, things have taken a serious turn for the worse.

An Expert's Opinion

Mr. and Mrs. Bing anxiously await the doctor's arrival. They pace back and forth in the girls' room trying to wrap their minds around what's happened. "Something strange is going on here. I mean, something weird is happenin' on this planet! First the sun goes missing and now Suzie's bones disappeared, too. It must be some consequence of the sun dyin' off yesterday. There must be other cases like this occurring throughout the whole wide world. Suzie can't be the only kid goin' through this," Mr. Bing declares out loud, mainly trying to work out the mystery in his own mind. When no answers magically reveal themselves, he declares, "I think the best thing to do is eat us some breakfast. You know Suzie's bones might come back. Everyone knows things have a way of takin' care of themselves. Remember last winter Ryder had that stomachache and the doctor wanted to run a bunch of expensive tests? Well, I knew they were just trying to charge us for the tests…so I didn't overreact and you know what, we didn't need them tests after all."

Ryder breaks in. "Seriously, Dad, you're not talking about the time you thought my stomachache would go away by itself and after three days of terrible cramps, my appendix burst? The time I was rushed by ambulance to the hospital for emergency surgery? Is that the incident you're talking about?"

"Yup, you bet it is. Those tests were worthless. When your appendix burst, we knew what the problem was. You got your surgery and we saved all the money from those doggone unnecessary tests. You can't trust them fancy doctor folk with their shiny white lab coats and hard-to-get degrees, they are just trying to rip you off so they can buy a new boat. Well, we showed them, didn't we?"

Ryder shakes her head. It's tough being the brains of the operation. "Dad, what difference did it make, anyway? You weren't going to pay the bill for the tests just like you didn't pay the bill for the ambulance or the hospital stay or the surgeon or…well, you get my point."

"Let's get back to the crisis at hand," Mrs. Bing says, staring at Suzie. "What I don't understand, young lady, is how you can be so careless with your bones. I'm sick to death of you always losing things. When you were little you lost your crayons, your shoes and your blankey. Now you've gone and lost your bones. I swear you have no respect for the sacrifices your father and I make. We struggle, sacrifice and scrimp so you can have nice things. How do you repay us? You go and lose all your bones. Do you think we are rich? That money grows on trees? We can just run out and buy new bones because you didn't keep up with your old ones?"

Even Mr. Bing is stunned by his wife's comment. "Honey, I might be wrong, but I don't think Suzie misplaced her bones. You're probably just hungry and a little bit on edge. She's tough to look at right now, I know. What I really think we need right now is a good, solid breakfast."

The back and forth chatter drives Suzie crazy. "Shut up," she hollers. "I'm glad you guys are interested in debating what caused my bones to vanish, but I'm not. My bladder is full and I can't move. I have a lot of problems over here and listening to your ugly voices isn't helping. Beyond that, can someone please get Mrs. Armstrong to shut off her weed eater? The loud hum from it is going to make me mad!"

Suzie's passionate outbursts are common in the Bing household, but she's never been this angry before. Ryder takes offense. "Sis, you don't have to shout. We're doing everything we can. The reason Daddy, Mama and I are discussing this is because we love you. We're trying to figure out how to help. Jumping down our throats about it isn't going to help find your bones. Or grow them back. Or whatever needs to happen to fix you."

"Let your sister shout if she wants," Mrs. Bing breaks in. "She has every right. Imagine how uncomfortable she must be in that soupy body of hers. That frenzied old piece of junk weed whacker is bugging me, too, and I'm as solid as a steel building. And you two aren't going to solve this puzzle by talking about it, so take Suzie's advice and shut up!" She marches from the room to tell the neighbor to shut off her old clunky machine.

*****

Dr. Meredith encounters an interesting sight when she pulls into the Bings' gravel driveway. Mrs. Bing stands across the street with a slice of pizza in one hand, the television remote in the other, screaming at a little old lady with an antique weed eater. Despite the interesting scenario playing out before the doctor's eyes, she remembers the real reason for her visit—Suzie's disappearing bone condition. When Mr. Bing telephoned her this morning, she highly doubted the authenticity of his call. An entire skeletal system doesn't evaporate. Had he called her last week, she would have dismissed his ranting as the disillusions of a hillbilly; however, yesterday the sun was pronounced dead, so today she feels more forgiving and less judgmental about the rules of life. After yesterday, anything is possible.

Fear strikes the old doctor as soon as she lays eyes on Suzie's condition. In forty-five years of practicing medicine, she's never seen anything like this before. The poor kid's body is limp and unstructured like a puddle of mud after a serious rainstorm. According to the rules of life, Suzie Bing shouldn't be alive in this condition. The human body is designed with a skeletal system for a reason—to protect the internal organs, to provide support to the structure and the bones themselves are important storage units for vital minerals and marrow.

"We must get Suzie to the nearest hospital right away," Dr. Meredith explains. "I have no idea what to do with her or how to treat her. Your observation certainly fits. Her body looks like the skeleton is gone. Yet, I can't be sure that's what's happened. Without a skeletal system, I don't know how we're going to transport her to the hospital. The skeleton protects the internal organs, including the heart and brain, from damage. If we move her, we could injure the most vital parts of her body. I need backup. I'm calling my dear friend Dr. Asher. He's an orthopedic surgeon—a bone doctor. If he can't figure out what to do, no one can."

*****

Hours later, a team of medical professionals are huddled around Suzie's twin bed, trying to diagnose her symptoms and develop a plan. Cats keep jumping onto the bed, interrupting the doctors. The animals rub themselves against the doctors' legs, hoping to steal attention away from the young patient. Finally, Dr. Asher loses his cool and orders the family to round up all the cats and get them out of the room. He can't work under these conditions and this is the most interesting case he's ever seen. "I can't concentrate with these blasted cats hovering around me like I'm a dead mouse. Get them out or I'm going to scream!"

Ryder grabs Milo, Pooter, Mickey and Dexter, tucking the cats under her arms and trying to hold them still long enough to get them out of the room. As soon as she leaves with them, Gizzer and Chester run into the bedroom to avoid capture in the living room. What follows next looks like a circus act. When two cats are removed from the bedroom, three more come in. It takes the Bing family twenty minutes before Boo, Gus, Sassy Pants, Monster Man, Snicker, Snuffer, Mickey, Stir Fry, Gizzer, Milo, Maxwell, Hokey, Pokey, Dexter, Smarty Pants, Winnie, Chester, Tuffy, Feather Asphalt and Pooter are eventually contained in the kitchen.

With the cats finally out of the way, Dr. Asher and his team examine Suzie. They check with hospitals around the world, searching for similar cases of medical mysteries following the sun's death and resurrection. So far, Suzie's case in Swampville, Florida, is the only incidence of its kind. The doctors are baffled by her extreme state, but they realize they must act fast to get her as comfortable and as safe as possible. Transporting her to the hospital, in her current condition, is impossible. Her internal organs can't handle the trip. An engineer is called in to design a "traveling suit" for her—something that will support her muscles and organs.

The nurses pump her full of minerals and antibiotics to keep her immune system healthy and fight infection. Her messy room is a far cry from the sterile environment of the hospital, but they do what they can. Everyone helps to scrub, bleach, clean and disinfect the bedroom. Soon, the girls' room looks more like a hazmat scene than a teenage hangout.

Thanks to a catheter, Suzie's bladder problem is remedied. No more urge to visit the toilet. Normally, doctors and nurses make Suzie uncomfortable. When she broke her foot two years ago, she hated the hospital because it was scary. Now, she feels comforted by the team of medical professionals who are working hard to keep her healthy. She's confident they'll find a way to fix her. Besides, bad things don't permanently happen to thirteen-year-old girls. "I don't care what you have to do to me, just don't leave," she says to Dr. Asher. At this point, shots in the arm are better than the fear of the unknown.

Ryder tries to keep Suzie upbeat. "Listen, think of it this way, you're the only girl in the whole world to have this. The doctors might even name a new disease after you. I can picture it now, having no backbone or foundation, being just a massive puddle of fatty tissue oozing toward the path of least resistance will be called The Suzie Bing Condition. The name Suzie R. Bing will become synonymous with the idea of fat blobs everywhere, blobs of talking, babbling people with no substance whatsoever." This conversation doesn't cheer the patient and Ryder soon finds herself in isolation, away from Suzie, with the cats in the kitchen.

Later in the day, a brilliant engineer arrives with his prototype bone suit he's labored to design quickly for Suzie's transportation to the hospital. The special invention is packaged inside a garment bag to protect the engineer's design from outside prying eyes. When he unzips the long garment bag and reveals his master creation, everyone is filled with shock. What he's created is a black human-shaped mold made from titanium to keep it lightweight. Suzie shivers, but is also intrigued. It looks like a Suzie-sized cookie cutter. She imagines the baking instructions: Grease pan, pour in patient, bake for forty-five minutes at 350 degrees and out will pop a perfect gingerbread Suzie. Before anyone can speak, Tuffy escapes the kitchen quarantine area through a hole in the back window screen. He runs around the house before expertly leaping through a hole in the screen of Suzie's room. He takes one look at the person-sized cake-pan suit, arches his back and hisses with contempt. When nurse Jackie tries to remove him, Tuffy hisses and stalks straight legged out of the room.

Unfazed by the cat's lack of confidence, the engineer explains the benefits of the suit's function. Since Suzie had always dreamed of being an astronaut, she didn't fear tight spaces. She liked to imagine what life might feel like in the small confines of a space ship. She knew these trips could be daunting, but spending time in this compressed body container appeared much worse than anything she imagined astronaut's face.

When Mrs. Bing voices her issues with the new Suzie suit, Dr. Asher quickly reassures her that the titanium stiffening body mold is the answer to her daughter's problems. What she needs is corrective support and this unusual concoction is the remedy. "Just think of it like a uniform for the boneless," he says, trying to dispel everyone's edgy nerves. His comment doesn't help. Dr. Asher has the bedside manner of an Artic blizzard. Unaware of the patient's growing hate for the new suit, he casually straightens his bow tie and waits for someone to react positively to his uplifting comment. Surprisingly only to him, no one does.

"No, this can't be happening to me," Suzie finally screams. "This can't be real. I'm not wearing that! There's no way. You can't make me. I would rather lie in bed than have that awful thing hooked around me!"

Ryder weaves her way back to the bedroom when she hears her sister's cries. "Would everyone leave us for a while so I can sit with Suzie alone? We need some sibling time to talk things out."

The room clears, leaving the two Bing daughters to commiserate in peace. Despite the two sisters' differences, deep down under their different-colored hair and different decorating styles they are best friends. Suzie explains her hatred of the skeleton tomb. Ryder lets her speak and doesn't argue. Suzie is right. The suit resembles something from a medieval torture chamber. If boiling in oil didn't work, this suit would have terrified any enemy. When Suzie stops talking, Ryder doesn't say anything. There's nothing she can say to make her little sister feel better. Instead, she looks at Suzie warmly and smiles. Together, they can get through anything.

Suzie breaks the silence. "I know what you're thinking. That anything is better than this bed. That I am not safe here exposed to the elements. I need to get to the hospital and the only way to do so is by wearing the titanium suit. And you're right, but I hate this. I hate being sick. It's not fun. I just want to be healthy again. I just want the rules to go back to normal."

"I know. Everything will be fine. I'm proud of you, Suzie-Q. I think you're awfully brave. Not many kids could handle this as well as you are. I know I couldn't. I'd be bawling my eyes out. But I do have to say, if you kind of close one eye and squint a little, it resembles a space suit like the astronauts wear. Plus, imagine how cool everyone will think you are for getting your own personalized bone suit. Not a single kid has that in school. If you tell Taylor it's couture, she'll give you every dime of her allowance to buy it off you."

"Get your camera. I'm going to need a picture of this. Once I post this bad-boy suit to my blog, no one at school will be able to forget me. The popular crowd will befriend me for sure."

"Why?" Ryder asks.

"Because they'll have the exclusive story about the girl with the titanium bone suit. I'll be a hero for surviving this ordeal. This has just secured my position in the 'it' crowd for the rest of junior high!"

Skeleton Mold

Getting Suzie into the metal suit is proving more challenging than the doctors expected. It would be easier to pour her into a large bucket. Her body wants to run in every direction, as soon as the doctors lift one side, everything runs to the opposite side. Their first attempt to place her feet in the mold first fails miserably. Both feet puddle together in one slot. With so much feet in one foot, the remaining tissue spills into the other foot slot creating a lot of nasty reactions. Nurse Barbara runs to the bathroom while her aide passes out and nearly knocks herself unconscious by hitting her head on the floor. Perhaps if they had allowed the pets to stay inside the bedroom, the aide's fall would have been cushioned by a soft, furry body.

When the foot-first mission is aborted, the doctors try next to insert Suzie's flattened head into the face portion of the skeleton suit. This works better than starting with the feet and soon they have a working start. Carefully, the team slides her body into the titanium mold. When the last layer of blubber is smoothed out, the engineer shuts the top portion of the suit over Suzie's body, locking it tightly on the side with a thick padlock. She immediately feels better.

For the first time since dawn, Suzie doesn't feel like she's going to slither onto the floor.

    The EMTs load her into the ambulance and head to the hospital. Unfortunately, no one notices her left ear stuck to her bedroom pillow like an abandoned wad of tissue.

Liquid

At the hospital, the doctors are still lost and clueless. They decide to keep her locked in the metal skeletal suit until they formulate a plan of attack. It's not ideal, but it beats worrying that she'll ooze off the hospital bed and run down the drain in the bathroom shower.

The night slowly ticks by. Since she can't use her hands, a liquid diet is ordered. Suzie sips her dinner through a thick straw stuck in a small hole in the suit over her mouth. It isn't a milkshake or a smoothie, but tastes like a pot roast with mashed potatoes and gravy has been spun through the blender until it was reduced to mere mush, then the cooks poured it into a glass, added a straw and called it dinner. The warm and lumpy chunks coming through the straw are disgusting. Sniffing the warm air inside her well-engineered box, she detects the sweet scent of candy bars. "Are you eating candy?" she asks, outraged. How could her family calmly munch chocolate at a time like this? If she has to eat mushy pot roast through a straw, the Bings could have the common decency to at least eat outside her room. "Hey, I asked a question. Do you think I can't smell in here? Because I can. See the two nose slots over the mouth slot?"

Mr. Bing shoves the remaining candy bar into his mouth. "Wa ya taing abou?" he asks, trying to hide the evidence.

"Really, Dad. At least swallow before you try to pretend you're not eating a candy bar," Suzie says.

Grabbing a soda to wash down the candy bar and prevent choking on the chocolaty delight, Mr. Bing says, "Sorry, sweetie, it's just that no one has eaten since breakfast. We were literally starving to death. Your mother was so weak she barely had the energy to make it to the vending machine. You have a nice tasty pot roast smoothie handed to you while we battled hunger pangs—it ain't fair. I don't think you understand how difficult this has been on us. You get to lie around in a nice custom-built body box while we have to endure these tiny, hard, uncomfortable chairs. Seriously, I think they were made for children. I haven't been able to feel my feet for hours. But do I complain? No, I do not. I sit here with my dead feet and starving belly handling this epic personal disaster like a real pro."

"Oh, Dad, just stop," Ryder breaks in. "Suzie, the cafeteria is closed and we were hungry. Want me to see if they have some pudding or Jell-O you can eat with your straw?"

"No. Don't bring up pudding or Jell-O at a time like this. Just remember this next time you are in a body box and I sit around eating candy bars."

"Deal," Ryder agrees.

*****

Together they pass the evening with family stories and by laughing at themselves yesterday for trying to fly to the Mall of America during a worldwide blackout. Even the idea of Wandy Vall and her strange questions causes them to burst into laughter. How funny, a reporter showing up on their front porch demanding answers for a local story. The Bings are clearly the last family in town to interview. Poor Miss Vall really was a novice. Her career wasn't likely to soar anytime soon. Finally, as night falls, Mr. and Mrs. Bing promise to take the family on a real vacation, somewhere natural—not manmade—when Suzie recovers. They discuss renting an RV for a cross-country road trip to Yellowstone National Park. Seeing bears rather than alligators would be a nice change. Yet, deep down, despite everyone's high spirits, they secretly fear Suzie will be stuck inside that suit for a long time.

Press Attacks

Suzie awakens to hundreds of strange faces staring at her through the window in her hospital door. News of her condition traveled fast. The night shift nurses couldn't wait to tell their friends about the strange girl with no bones admitted in a spooky metal suit. Those friends, in turn, couldn't wait to tell their friends. Soon the media was contacted. Wandy Vall heard the story from her roommate at two o'clock in the morning. She immediately recognized Suzie's name and realized she knew the family. Without hesitation, the young intern gathered her notes, her pocket-sized camcorder and rushed to the hospital to cover the story. Luck was on Wandy's side because Dr. Asher and Dr. Meredith were all too happy to reach out to the medical community at large for answers to Suzie's mysterious condition. Miss Vall poufed her hair, dabbed a second coat of lipstick, straightened her inexpensive suit and donned her most emotive face as she introduced the story to the world. She explained with great concern the difficult plight poor Suzie Bing's body was in without the structure and stability of her skeletal system. Dr. Asher and Dr. Meredith urged any doctor with knowledge of this rare disease to contact them immediately. Wandy Vall ended her powerful interview by saying with a wobbling lip, "Ladies and gentleman, a brave little girl needs our help. It will take the global medical community acting together or it might take a single rare genius, but together we can find a cure and save this little girl. I'm Wandy Vall reporting from Swampville Children's Hospital, channel nineteen news."

  Hoping to get the story to go national, Wandy Vall quickly calls her affiliate station in New York and explains the story. They want the story covered by actual pros and send reporters out on the next flight to Florida. By seven a.m., the local and national news have sent a barrage of reporters to learn everything they can about the girl with no bones. The hospital is suddenly full of people from all over the United States hoping to catch a glimpse of the odd makeshift bone suit and the little girl trapped inside. Headline ideas scurry around like ants at a picnic: BONES BE GONE, TITANIUM SKELETON SUIT SAVES FLORIDA GIRL FROM DEATH, FIRST NO SUN, NOW NO BONES, WHAT'S NEXT?

  "I think I have company," Suzie says, looking out the window from the small eye-slot in her mask. She tries to turn her head but her suit is too tight. She can't budge inside it. Gone are the swooshing sounds her skin made as it sloshed around the sectioned off crevices of her bone box. She tries to wiggle her toes, then her fingers. Finally, she screams, "Get me out of this thing!"

Mr. and Mrs. Bing are too busy smiling for the cameras to notice their daughter's pleas. Ignoring the mob outside, Ryder rushes to Suzie's side. Even encased in the metal suit, Ryder can tell her sister is better. Something must have happened overnight. Under the eye slats are two perfectly round eyes blinking at her with annoyance. Her nostrils poke out the nose holes, her lips brush through the hole where the straw fed her dinner. Last night, her features weren't visible. Occasionally, an eye would roll past the upper slit like a beach ball in the pool, but now, her eyes stay firmly in place. Could Suzie's form have returned as quickly as it disappeared?

Ryder wades through the crowd of visitors searching for Dr. Asher and Dr. Meredith. Finally she spies them and waves them over. "You've got to see this," she exclaims, bursting back through Suzie's hospital room door. At first glance, they know she's better, too.

"I think we've made improvement," Dr. Asher announces proudly like the hero who saved the day. "Let's unlock the chamber and see how things look underneath." To everyone's delight, he finds Suzie completely intact. The mob outside can no longer be contained and reporters break down the door to get a peek at the mysterious bone disappearing disease. Cameras are rolling long before anyone realizes there is no show to see. Suzie looks exactly like every other chubby, dark-haired thirteen-year-old girl with crooked teeth on the planet. She isn't a puddle of human flesh at all. The reporters are mad. Real mad. They demand answers. Why did the doctors deceive them?

Dr. Asher faces the media attacks with professionalism. He schedules a press conference in twenty minutes, calls security to usher the crowd from Suzie's bedside and attempts to clear his thoughts while tending to his patient before making a final statement. Despite a heavy interrogation and barrage of questions from the Bing family, he has no answers for them. Yesterday, Suzie's bones were clearly missing and today they've returned. While examining her for release back home, he pulls the hair back around her face and discovers her missing ear — the last and only remaining symptom from a day without bones. He isn't worried and explains that he can reattach the ear should they find it at home, assuming of course, the cats don't find it first.

After he leaves, Mrs. Bing turns on the television, hoping to watch the hype about Suzie's condition. Instead, she reads the headline: WHERE ARE THE ANIMALS? "What animals? What is all this about? Why aren't you the main story? What could be more interesting than losing your skeleton and gaining it back again?" She isn't happy about her daughter missing her fifteen minutes of fame over a boring story about missing animals. This was Suzie's time to shine. Didn't the news understand that? Ryder, however, realizes how significant the headline must be if it's trumped her sister's condition. "Turn it up, Mama, this might be important."

A skinny lady reports, "This may be the freakiest week on record. Saturday, the sun died. Sunday, it returned. And today, Monday, the animals have disappeared. No one has seen a single animal since midnight. Pets are missing, zoo animals are gone, squirrels aren't running through the parks and this is the case all over the world. Even the animals we've tagged with trackers have disappeared. Their trackers are still active, but unable to explain what happened to every furry creature on Earth."

*****

Dr. Asher stands in front of the amassed group attempting to explain how yesterday Suzie Bing had a rare and life-threatening condition and today she presents without symptoms. The press doesn't believe his miraculous story. They accuse him of making up the condition for his personal gain and reputation in the orthopedic world. While other reporters harass the antiquated man, Wandy Vall leaves the press conference. She's on a mission to find Suzie and ask her directly what happened. Wandy can't understand why the reporters are acting defensively about the story. Only two days ago, the sun didn't rise and now every animal on Earth is missing. To her, strange things are happening and she wants to get to the bottom of the story. Besides, a candid one-on-one interview with Suzie Bing wouldn't be a bad career move either way. Either the doctor made it all up and the story can be spun as a child victimization case or the doctor is telling the truth and it's a miracle. And miracle stories always get great coverage. Wandy re-poufs her hair and pinches her slender cheeks. One way or another, her story is going national.

Wandy taps lightly on Suzie's hospital door. Mr. Bing is happy to see the perky redhead and waves her inside. "So, I've heard a lot of competing stories about what happened here yesterday. Would you mind giving me an exclusive scoop?" the young reporter inquires.

Mrs. Bing isn't impressed by the intern's good looks and boldly believes it's time for reporters to leave her family alone. Then an idea strikes her. An idea that might save her from resume writing for a while. "Whatcha payin'?"

Wandy is caught off guard. She wasn't expecting the family to demand payment for their story. "I'm not here to offer you anything except the ability to tell the nation the truth about what happened yesterday. They are concerned about Suzie and want to know if she nearly died or if she was used for the cruel purposes of advancing Dr. Asher's career."

"Well, Beulah, I don't think it is right not to tell the good people what they want to know," Mr. Bing explains to his wife, hoping the nice reporter lady won't get offended and leave.

Mrs. Bing isn't interested in the truth. She's interested in earning enough money to take her daughter on the vacation she promised. In her mind, Suzie deserves a trip to Yellowstone National Park and settling for the truth instead of a payday isn't an acceptable strategy. Suddenly, she envisions her own television show on the CARE network like the reality show *Mark and Jen plus ten*. Or was it *Jen and Mark live in an Ark*? Either way, Suzie would make a great star. She has the unique look of a Hollywood actress. If they play this right, maybe a hit television show is the next step for the family.

Wandy continues to explain the importance of reassuring the American people. She's getting nowhere with the parents so she decides to appeal to Suzie. Walking to the edge of her bed, she asks, "Suzie, did you have bones yesterday?"

Cast Away Critters

"Don't you answer her, girl," Mrs. Bing warns before hitting the emergency button on the wall and signaling the nurse. Barbara arrives post haste and shoos the bold reporter from the room before Suzie has a chance to answer. The discharge papers are ready. It's time to go home. Wandy doesn't have a choice. She leaves in defeat. No headline story for her today. Her cellphone beeps. It's her boss. He wants her to cover the situation at the park and do a small story on the disappearance of Jim, the happy tree squirrel everyone feeds buttercup bars to on their lunch breaks. Wandy groans. Life as a news intern isn't working out the way she'd hoped. Boneless hillbillies make good stories; missing squirrels do not.

*****

Though the air inside the house smells fresher, coming home to a cat-free house upsets the Bing family terribly. Boo, Gus, Sassy Pants, Monster Man, Snicker, Snuffer, Mickey, Stir Fry, Gizzer, Milo, Maxwell, Hokey, Pokey, Smarty Pants, Dexter, Winnie, Chester, Tuffy, Feather, Asphalt and Pooter are gone. Cat fur sticks to every surface, framed cat pictures hang on the walls and litter boxes putrefy the air, but no real cats are there to greet them. Suzie slumps down in the oversized sofa and sighs. "Do you think they will return tomorrow?"

"Why would they?" Mrs. Bing asks.

"Because the sun was only gone one day. My bones were only gone one day. Why should the animals be gone longer than that?"

Ryder thinks her sister has a point. "She's right. These strange events only occur for a single day. Whatever is happening around here, doesn't last long. We just have to wait until tomorrow and our furry friends will return to us."

"But where are they now?"

"Wherever the sun and Suzie's bones went."

"Why was I the only person to lose my bones yesterday, why me?"

"I don't know." Ryder tries to think of a reason to appease her sister. "There's only one explanation: you're as special and important as the sun.

"That's not it. I'm beginning to wonder if all of this is happening to teach me a lesson."

"A lesson about what?"

"A lesson about how important the rules are. Without them, everything goes awry. Nothing makes sense and everything is in danger. I don't like this. I want everything to return to normal. If this is a lesson, then I get it. I understand now why we need rules. I don't want to go through any more weird days—days without the sun, or bones or Boo, Gus, Sassy Pants, Monster Man, Snicker, Snuffer, Mickey, Dexter, Stir Fry, Gizzer, Milo, Maxwell, Hokey, Pokey, Smarty Pants, Chester, Tuffy, Feather, Asphalt and Pooter."

"What about Winnie?" Ryder asks.

"Yes, and Winnie. Winnie's my favorite. I can't believe I forgot Winnie!"

Random Consequences

Wednesday morning greets the Bings with a sunny sky and bony bodies. Suzie throws the quilt from her bed and rushes to find Snuffer, her second favorite kitty. There's no sign of her anywhere. The cats haven't returned. Suzie wails with distress and flips on the television to learn whether it's just her pets that are still missing or all the animals of the world. She waits for the TV to click on but nothing happens. She presses the ON button again. This time the microwave springs to life, the light inside switches on and the turntable begins slowly turning. Although Suzie uses the microwave nearly every day, the noise frightens her. Ryder hears the commotion and starts lecturing her little sister on the danger of using the microwave when there's nothing inside. Ryder slams the microwave door shut. This triggers the ceiling fan in the living room to begin whirling at top speed. Suzie watches the ceiling fan dance with wild momentum. "Ryder, something else is wrong. I didn't start the microwave. The TV won't work and now the fan is racing out of control."

The girls try to shut off the ceiling fan, but their actions inadvertently turn on the shower, turn off the air conditioning and cause a purple beehive to magically appear swarming on a pot atop the stove. Frantic to get rid of the hive, they holler for their parents.

Mr. and Mrs. Bing have the same unpredictable luck. Mr. Bing dons oven mitts and carefully lifts the swarming hive. Honey bees sting his arms, face and hands. He prepares for the awful pain their stingers pack, but to his relief, their stingers don't cause him any grief. Instead, they feel like little massages from a tiny expert masseuse. He makes it to the front porch and is ready to toss the hive into the yard when the hive turns into a rose bush with lovely red blossoms. He rather likes the bush and decides to bring it back inside. The flowers smell heavenly—almost like pancakes covered in maple syrup. Mesmerized by the fragrant bush, the Bings stop everything to smell the roses.

Eventually, some unaccounted for action in the Bing household triggers the radio. The current news story blares from the small device hidden under the sofa, lost for nearly two years before its recent recovery. "I don't know if this missive will reach our intended audience, however, we must try. This is the most unusual day we've seen to date. It appears our actions have random consequences. As the gentleman continues to explain the odd events, his voice turns into the sound of a rooster crowing and his message is lost on human ears. However, the rose bush seems to understand and panics, quickly lifting its underbrush and scurrying away to hide under the sofa with the radio. Unbelievably, the bush fits, though there's no physics equation that could explain why.

"What is happening to our world?" Mrs. Bing cries with confusion.

"It's the end of the world as we know it," Mr. Bing shouts, unaware he's quoting a famous song chorus.

"It's not the end of the world!" Ryder snaps. "Something is causing this weird stuff to happen. We just have to figure out what that is and fix it."

"It's me. I'm the one causing this mess," Suzie answers. "If I hadn't been so sure that rules were bad, none of this would be happening right now."

"Talk about the spotlight effect." Ryder sighs, using her new fascination with social psychology as a reference point. "I'm pretty sure this glitch doesn't have anything to do with you."

"I don't know. She is the only one who lost her bones," Mr. Bing points out. The more he considers Suzie's point, the more he fears she may be correct. Besides, to him, his daughters are as important as the sun so he sees nothing illogical about the connection.

Their heated conversation is interrupted by a loud thud down the hall. The family rushes to find the source of the noise. In the middle of the hall, they find a large crate with crying sounds wailing within. Suzie pries the crate open with her bare hands. Apparently, the unusual events of the day have also endowed her with massive strength.

Inside, she finds an infant covered in pink feathers. "Oh no, it's a human-flamingo-hybrid baby," she screams.

Mrs. Bing pulls the tot from the crate and examines it from head to toe. Somewhat sadly she says, "It's not a human-flamingo-hybrid baby. See, the feathers wipe right off. He looks fine. In fact, some might even call him perfect. That is of course if such a concept existed in reality, rather than in the purely intellectual world of philosophy and aesthetics."

Stunned by his wife's comment, Mr. Bing blurts out, "There is certainly something odd about today. Anyone care for breakfast?"

"So *that's* where babies come from," Ryder exclaims. "How exciting! We have a new brother."

"And you're supposed to be the smart one in the family," Suzie exclaims. "Babies don't come from hall crates, you dummy, they come from storks. Clearly he isn't our brother. Duh."

Mrs. Bing holds the new babe happily. "He's beautiful, and look at that smile," she says, staring into his big brown eyes with the gushing joy of a new mother. "What shall we name him?"

Mr. Bing peers into the child's small, glowing face. "I like the name Samson. Had a cat one time named Samson. He was a fine cat. Let's call him Sam."

"Am I the only one who thinks we can't keep him?" Suzie asks. "I hate to interrupt a precious family moment, but he's not ours. We can't just name him, stick a bib on him and call him a Bing.

"He has a name now," Mr. Bing replies. "And of course we can keep Sam. He fits right in; he's your brother."

"Not to point out the obvious, but he doesn't fit right in. Not exactly. He's black," Suzie shouts.

"No one will notice a tiny detail like that," Mrs. Bing says. "Besides, I've been known to get pretty dark in the summers. Mark my word, he'll fit like another sardine on a pepperoni pizza." Ryder shakes her head, trying to decipher her father's strange expression.

"Yeah, Beulah, remember that time in Mexico?" Mr. Bing says with a smile. The adults chuckle, remembering their honeymoon, and for a moment completely forget the issues at hand. Their daughters ignore them. Whenever the Bings' honeymoon is mentioned, both parents disappear into a fog of past times. Ryder and Suzie wait for them to return to the present.

They don't return though, as they stand there holding their new son, reminiscing about old times. Finally, Ryder interrupts their personal moment. "Hey, what are we going to do? How can we do anything when we don't know the consequences of what will happen? I turn on the light switch and a baby in a box falls through the roof. This is a big deal. We need to think of a plan."

Mr. and Mrs. Bing are too caught up in Sam's tiny features to pay their eldest daughter much attention. Despite the uncertainty of the day, they are having a wonderful time. What's not to like? So far the day's brought them a nice battery-operated radio, a swarm of massaging bees, a beautiful walking rose bush and a baby boy. It's not every day you get a new family member and a prized ruby red Lincoln rose. "I'm going up to the attic to find Sam some clothes. Hopefully, we have something from the girls that isn't too frilly for him," Beulah Bing states, handing off her new little man to Mr. Bing.

Suzie scratches the hole on the side of her face where her ear once was. She agrees with Ryder. They need a plan to get through this day before they end up with seven new brothers. "So I really think I'm the one to blame for all these strange occurrences. It was my thick-headedness that caused this. If I had only seen the value of rules and not been such a smarty pants about the issue, everything would be fine right now. I'd still have my ear, we wouldn't have Sam. Gus, Boo, Sassy Pants, Monster Man, Snicker, Snuffer, Mickey, Stir Fry, Gizzer, Milo, Maxwell, Hokey, Pokey, Chester, Tuffy, Dexter, Feather, Asphalt and Pooter would still be here and Dr. Asher wouldn't be facing angry mobs of reporters."

"You forgot Winnie again."

"Oops, sorry, Winnie. Wherever you are, little buddy, I love you."

"Okay, I'll play along with you for a minute," Ryder says, finally giving her sister's thought some credit. "Let's say you did put this weirdness in motion, what did you do to cause it? Simply believing in something doesn't have effects like this, so you must have done something to make this happen."

"I did. I looked at the sky, put my fist in the air and said, 'Rules are stupid.' "

"Yeah, I don't think that is powerful enough to make an impact like this. Did anything else strange occur?"

"The tornado. The tornado happened as soon as I shook my fist at the clouds. And now that I think about it, there was a really strange cloud in the sky. It looked almost like a star. It was white and puffy, but had five long points that made it seem like a stretched-out star."

"Maybe the cloud counted as a wish on a shooting star," Ryder replies. "But seriously, Suzie, you can't honestly think you had anything to do with the strangest week of life on Earth."

"That's exactly what I think. You heard Daddy. He believes I'm to blame. Granted, he also believes in Big Foot, that area fifty-one is an alien landing base, and that he will one day catch a world record bass and get his own cable TV fishing show, so he may not be the best character reference.

Now, let's stop all this gibber-jabbering and figure out how to get our world back to normal."

"It's simple. We don't need a plan, just go outside and make a fist. Apparently your magic will change everything," Ryder jokes. Suzie doesn't laugh. Ryder may have been joking, but her idea seems as plausible as anything else happening this week. Suzie decides to follow Ryder's advice and wanders outside, careful to avoid anything that might trigger an unnatural consequence. Although Mr. Bing said the bee stings felt like tiny fists rubbing his sore muscles, she doesn't want to do anything to bring back the purple hive again. Looking up at the sky, she finds another surprise. The clouds aren't clouds today at all; they are wooden rocking chairs breezing through the sky like airplanes.

"I can't wish upon a rocking chair," she mutters with disappointment. So much for her attempt at correcting the chaos around them.

"Guess your magic fist won't work today," Ryder jokes again, admiring the rocking chairs tumbling through the sky. "Let's go exploring. I think today is the perfect day for that picnic down by the lake. Who knows what we'll see. Any day where rocking chairs are clouds, is a day worth exploring."

Suzie reluctantly agrees. Shaking her fist at chairs doesn't seem helpful. She is hungry and probably not the cause of the strange week anyway. A little sightseeing and lunch by the lake won't cause any problems. She hopes.

The Lake

Mr. and Mrs. Bing are too interested in dressing Sam in a pair of little coveralls to worry much about their daughters picnicking on the lake during such an odd day. Other parents would panic if crates with babies, rocking chairs for clouds and rooster crowing news reporters happened. They would fear that the lake would be a super highway instead or that their daughters might get sucked up into the strange sky only to be spun around and then land in someone else's hallway naked and covered in pink feathers. But not Mr. and Mrs. Bing. So the girls make themselves rice and bean sandwiches on bagels and head to the lake.

Strolling through a forest without animals is unnerving. The birds sang. The crickets chirped. But the normal rabbit, squirrel and chipmunk sightings were a thing of the past. Eventually, their long hike brings them to their favorite old wooden picnic table in front of the lake. The area is empty. The entire park is theirs alone. In fashion with the rest of the day, the barren, tired wooden table is now a table fit for royalty. Its glass top glistens with the sun's powerful rays, its golden placemats shine and its bounty of food induces drool even in the most well-behaved diner.

Ryder and Suzie toss their sack of bean and rice sandwiches to the ground and take a seat on the rich velvety cushions. Fine china lines the table with handspun fabric linens for napkins. Suzie grabs a plate, real silverware, a napkin monogrammed TNR and begins piling on the decadent entrees. First, she takes a spoonful of au gratin potatoes, then a bit of French-style green beans, a piece of roasted trout and a heap of candied yams. Grabbing another plate for dessert, she adds a piece of chocolate cake, a slice of pecan pie and a tiny bowl of vanilla custard. This is the best picnic of her life. Ryder was right, it is a great day for exploring.

With ravenous hunger, Ryder digs into her plate of spaghetti and meatballs. The first bite sends her gagging away from the table. She spits her bite into the lake, choking on the taste. It tastes like potato soup. Big meaty balls of potato soup! Rubbing her tongue with her hand, she attempts to get every taste bud clean. "I guess we should have known there was a problem with the food when no ants were even interested," she says, finally satisfied her pallet is cleansed.

Across the table, Suzie is choking on her own soupy meal. Once the awful taste is out of her mouth, she begins searching for the sack of sandwiches she threw on the ground when they saw the smorgasbord on the king-inspired table. Rice and beans on bagels sounds pretty good after the potato soup fiasco.

But, of course, on a day like today, with no rules or reason, the sandwiches are gone. There's no trace of them. The girls decide to take a dip in the lake since eating is now out of the question. Luckily, the lake looks normal—just a refreshing blue pool of clear water, ideal for an afternoon swim. Besides, they figure it's better to brave the lake than sit at the table hungry, batting away the giant Florida mosquitos.

"We can't just jump in," Ryder says. "The water looks fine, but the food looked delicious, so we can't trust our eyes. The girls slowly ease themselves toward the lake's edge. Suzie dips her big toe into the chilly water. So far so good. It's water, it's deep and it's not too cold. Their bodies will adjust quickly. It feels fine. Boldly, they jump in and swim out several feet into the warmer part of the lake.

Ryder and Suzie soon forget their suspicions and paddle around, splashing one another and hunting for clam shells with their feet digging into the mucky sand below. Suddenly, out of nowhere, something big rubs against Suzie's leg. The creature's spiny features prick her skin. She jumps halfway out of her body, screaming and slapping the surface of the lake, sending sprays of water everywhere. Swimming as fast as her chubby arms will carry her, she races for the shore. Ryder reacts with annoyance and hollers after her sister, "What's wrong? Suzie-Q, what happened?"

With a rapid breath Suzie says, "Something is after me. It's big and I have to get out of here." She paddles to the shore, but she isn't fast enough to outrun the monster hot on her trail. It's after her and there's nowhere for her to go.

Weird Effects

A scaly crocodile pops his head out of the water. He's ugly, with thick green skin and bulging yellow eyes. He opens his mouth wide. Suzie snaps her eyes shut, waiting for his giant claws to rip into her flesh. Nothing happens. The crocodile clears his throat, then says, "I'm Rufus. You'll have to excuse me if I frightened you, but I seem to be a bit lost. Only moments ago, I was swimming in the ocean off Sanibel Island and now I'm here. Wherever here is. Again, I'm terribly sorry to frighten you."

Suzie is more amazed by his speech than by his appearance in the lake. "You speak?" she asks, thinking she's definitely lost her mind. Animals don't talk. Well, parrots talk and technically some apes talk through sign languages, but she's never heard of an orating crocodile.

"Here we go again. I just had this conversation with a boy from Texas named Chase. He fell in love with a mermaid and needed my help, but I guess none of that really matters now. Yes, I speak. I don't know why you humans think you're the only ones capable of a little gab fest here and there. What's more important than my ability to communicate is this strange week we're having. I'm not a young crocodile anymore. Believe me, I've seen a lot so I don't surprise easily, but I've never seen anything like this before. Half of my friends just vanished overnight and I can't find them anywhere."

Ryder swims over to their guest in amazement. "So you can speak English every day? Not just today? This isn't part of the glitch?"

"Yes, my speech is not the issue here. My location is the problem. I need to get back to my ocean and back to Sanibel Island. This place looks a little…" Rufus spins his head left and right, taking in the sights of the park, "…looks a little, um, less beachy than I prefer."

"Yeah, you're in the redneck woods now, Rufus. This is Swampville."

"So I gathered," he says, clearing his throat again.

"I'm sorry, I don't know any way to help you. Our cats disappeared and we still can't find them. It seems we can't control the unpredictability. We're victims of chance this week just like you and your missing friends," Ryder explains.

"Well, I am certainly not a victim. I make my own destiny. I don't believe in luck or chance. I like to steer my own ship, if you know what I mean," Rufus says. "All I have to do is find my way home and from there, I can fix the rest."

"What if you get home and immediately transport back here?" Suzie asks. "I don't think you want to expend all the effort of getting home only to end up back in the same place again. And besides, I think you'd make a cute pet. How do you feel about cats, and bean and rice sandwiches?"

Now Rufus is the one frightened. "First off, little lady, I am not a pet. Although I have never eaten a cat, bean and rice sandwich…"

"No, how do you feel about cats and how do you feel about bean and rice sandwiches?"

"Yes, that makes more sense. I don't eat sandwiches; however, I think I feel the same as any civilized being would about a rice and bean sandwich. I eat bad animals after they've been sentenced to death for their crimes. Sandwiches don't commit crimes. Although, I think an argument could be made that a rice and bean sandwich might be considered a culinary crime. But alas, I am not in charge of those. And, if I must, I will spend the rest of my days getting back to Sanibel Island. It's my home and nothing will stop me from trying. My friends are there. The biting midges are there. Shells of every imaginable shape are there. Like I said before, I make my own destiny. This crazy world can send me to Timbuktu and I'll still find my way home again."

Ryder is impressed with the crocodile's convictions. He seems like a straight-up nice guy with good principles. He's her kind of reptile. "Well, Rufus, I wish you all the luck in the world. I would head west, if I were you."

"Then west it is. Thank you, ladies. It was nice meeting you and I hope you find your cats soon, although I find them arrogant, vile and disgusting creatures. Their curiosity gets them in trouble often with the law, so I find them on my menu often. They aren't bad stir-fried." With that, he swims west, determined to find his missing friends and get back home.

*****

On the way back to the house, the girls stop to catch their breath. The humidity is higher than normal, even for Florida. They sip warm water from the bottles attached to their bikes and talk about Rufus. Right in the middle of their conversation, their two bikes turn into one huge sports car. It's a convertible with deep bucket seats and a shiny red exterior. A black leather-wrapped steering wheel and dashboard ablaze with fancy buttons arouses the girls' interest. Suzie hops behind the wheel with excitement. "This is awesome. If our parents get a baby, it's only fitting that we get a car!"

Ryder isn't excited at all. She knows Suzie is the last person on Earth who should be driving. She sighs with frustration. "Now we have to walk home and it's getting late. Mama is going to be angry."

"Walk? Are you kidding me? We aren't going to walk! I'm going to drive this bad boy home and the time certainly isn't a problem in this. It looks fast!" She turns the ignition key and revs the engine. Her short, stubby legs barely reach the pedals so she scoots down in the seat and instructs Ryder to watch the road for her. As she puts the car in drive, the steering wheel turns into a giant soccer ball with a smiley face looking right at her. Suzie isn't fazed; she slams on the gas and heads for home.

The car speeds backward out of control. Suzie can't maintain the wheel or the speed. Ryder screams at the top of her lungs for Suzie to brake, but the brakes won't work. They fly backward, barely missing a large tree before the sports car finally begins to react normally. It stops speeding backward, turns around one hundred and eighty degrees and roars forward with new gusto. They are headed in the wrong direction for home and they are going way too fast. The car careens toward the lake and crashes into the water, coming to a halt once it's completely submerged.

Ryder's nerves have run away without her. Now they are going to be even later. She told Suzie to walk, but her stubborn sister never listens. She doesn't utter a word as she swims out the top of the car and floats to shore. Suzie hates when Ryder is mad at her. "Please don't be upset. It's not my fault. Mama will understand. It's not like she doesn't realize this day has strange consequences. Let's not tell her about the car, per se, but let her know we were on our way home when something blocked our path. We can use Rufus and tell her he wouldn't let us pass and that's why we got delayed."

"You want to pawn this off on Rufus? Have you learned nothing about the consequences of bad decisions? You think this week is happening because you hate rules and yet you've learned nothing! If you didn't hate rules, didn't lie every chance you get and just accepted the consequences of your behavior, maybe the whole world wouldn't be suffering right now. Our cats wouldn't be missing, Sam wouldn't be a new part of the family and Rufus wouldn't be trucking himself back to his island home right now. Did you see how short his legs are? Can you imagine how long it will take to walk to Sanibel on those short little things? You are so frustrating, Suzie. Grow up!" Ryder doesn't say another word the remainder of the way home. When they finally reach the old hovel, the front porch light is aglow, reminding the girls they are late and their parents will be waiting for them, switches in hand.

Mr. and Mrs. Bing aren't waiting inside to punish the girls, though. They aren't even home. Ryder calls through the house, "Daddy? Mama? Sam?" Nothing. Total silence. "If our parents are missing, too, because of your stubbornness, I'm going to…"

"So you do believe this is my fault?" Suzie asks.

"Surprise," Mr. and Mrs. Bing shout in unison with Aunt Birdie's delayed 'surprise' coming shortly after theirs. Mr. and Mrs. Bing climb out from under the table. Aunt Birdie steps out of the pantry with baby Sam. "We decided to throw you a party," Auntie Birdie says. She grabs a poorly decorated cake from the stove and dances around the kitchen. The cake is still in the original baking pan. The icing is melted and whatever design it once possessed has smeared into a blob of random colors.

"Why are you throwing us a party?" Ryder asks, totally confused.

"Because you missed your curfew by over an hour. And in this house when you defy our authority and misbehave like that, we reward it," Mrs. Bing answers before blowing hard into a streamer horn.

Suzie beams from ear to her missing ear's hole. "See, Ryder, sometimes the bad decisions actually pay off." She slips into the kitchen to cut a piece of curfew-breaking cake.

"Yeah, one time in the history of the world doesn't count Suzie," Ryder yells, stomping down the hall to her bedroom. Sam's birthing crate is still in the way. She glances inside it to make sure a new baby hasn't arrived, before entering her room and slamming the door. She's had more than enough of this day and she won't celebrate its randomness by eating cake. In real life, you can't have your cake and eat it, too!

Slavery

Thursday morning looks unsuspecting enough. The sun is out. Gus, Boo, Sassy Paws, Monster Man, Snicker, Snuffer, Mickey, Stir Fry, Gizzer, Milo, Maxwell, Hokey, Pokey, Smarty Pants, Dexter, Winnie, Chester, Tuffy, Feather, Asphalt and Pooter are back. Suzie's bones are in place and switching on the lights once again has the right effect. Ryder wanders into her parents' room to tell them the good news, but to her surprise, they are standing over her old cradle making googly-goo noises. Surely, the baby is gone, too. He's not. She peers into the tiny crib and comes eye to eye with her new little brother. Apparently, he's not going anywhere. Much like Suzie's lost ear, Sam is an ongoing side effect of a random week.

A loud knock at the front door stirs everyone's attention. Suzie answers and finds a tall man barking orders. He wants to know why they aren't tending the orchards. He carries a long whip and promises to use it if Suzie and her family don't get outside and get to work at once.

Puzzled, Suzie says, "I'm sorry, sir, I have no idea what you're talking about. Perhaps you have the wrong house."

Her comment angers the tall man further. He doesn't understand why his slave is back-talking and hollers for the girl's mother. He isn't a completely cruel slave owner, he only punishes the adults for their children's sassy answers. Mrs. Bing waddles to the door expecting to see her sister, Birdie. This man isn't a pleasant sight. She knows immediately he brings trouble.

"Listen here, I want you and your family out working in ten minutes or there's going to be a mighty steep price to pay. You understand?" Mrs. Bing doesn't, but knows the right answer isn't no. She nods her head yes, closes the door and orders a family meeting.

"Turn on the radio," she orders. "I have a bad feeling that we're in for another strange day!"

Ryder follows her mother's serious instructions and finds an a.m. channel. An old man's gnarled voice booms forth. "This is an emergency. It appears that some people have no memory of the constitution as it was written over two hundred years ago. Our country has lost the principle on which it was founded. We are in trouble. The rules, laws, bill of rights and mandates that governed this fine and exemplary country are gone. Half of the population doesn't even remember the laws. The half that do remember are slowly losing their memories and are growing foggier on the subject by the minute. Those of us who didn't awaken as slaves are the lucky ones. Thousands of families awoke this morning to find themselves shackled to owners who demanded immediate labor and offered little in the way of food, shelter, kindness or medical aid. If you've found yourself a slave today, please do not try to run. Several innocent people have already been killed or imprisoned for doing so. Obey your master. I know and understand this is a difficult request, but we must protect you until we can get a better system in place. Congress is already working to change the rules while our citizens still remember what the constitution said in the first place. For those of us who awoke to find ourselves owners, please release your slaves, give them their freedom and authorize their independence. I'm William Burch. Please stand by as we get through this chaotic and frantic time together."

  The news program goes to commercial while the Bings stand around their radio, scratching their heads, trying to imagine what life without the United States

Constitution will be like. Ryder is the first to speak. "So today we're slaves. We have to do what the guy on the radio said. We have to do our jobs today and keep quiet. Rebelling won't help. The only thing we can do is get to work."

Suzie starts to protest, but her mother silences her. "Your sister is right. Today we're slaves. We can't run. We can't change our fate. We are powerless. We ain't even considered people today. I don't know what happened or what changed, but it's as if the last two hundred years of progressive movements and civil rights never did happen. Rather than abolishing slavery altogether, it looks like without the constitution, slavery grew more common. I guess we should have been more grateful to work for pay when we had the chance. Our lack of financial independence has finally cost us our freedom completely."

Mrs. Bing makes a sling for Sam out of a blanket and ties him to her body so she can care for him while she works. He happily murmurs, totally unaware of the plight his new family faces. She heats a bottle for him on the stove hurrying quickly. The idea of working all day for no money doesn't make her happy. She's angry, but powerless. "I hope them people in congress get this mess all figured out before I have to spend another day rushin' around the house with my new son like a mad woman. I shouldn't have to do anything today anyway. I'm a new mother. I have rights!"

Suzie doesn't understand Mrs. Bing's issue. "Mama, you didn't give birth to Sam. You're fine. If you whine to the slave driver, we'll all be in trouble."

Moments later, Mr. Bing opens the front door of his little hovel and discovers an orchard. The grove of luscious orange trees before him is gorgeous and smells delicious. White blossoms on the trees radiate a warm fragrance, sweetening the swampy air. It's a perfect Florida day. He's ready to enjoy the sunshine and orchard. Then he remembers… he's the one who has to pick the fruit. He's in for a long day of manual labor.

The Blasted Rosenberg

Mrs. Bing waddles outside and surveys her new position in life. It isn't pretty. Hundreds of her neighbors are already working the land, picking oranges and carrying huge crates of fruit to large trucks that will take the citrus into town to sell. The heat and humidity consume her at once. Sweat dots her wrinkled brow. Sam begins to cry. Mr. Rosenberg, the slave driver, is on her immediately.

"Do you think you have the right to stand around sweating like a pig in my orchard?"

Beulah Bing looks at him, trying to decide if running is completely out of the question. She loathes work. Especially work that is hot, dirty, hard and unpaid. This isn't her cup of tea. Or in this case, her glass of orange juice. "I ain't doin' this," she cries. "I have a baby to care for. He needs me. And besides, my body ain't built for this type of labor."

The slave driver studies her obese frame. You can tell from his eyes that he agrees with her. "I can see that," he says. "I'll tell you what, I might be able to find another place for you. Follow me."

Mrs. Bing grins toward her family. She's proud of herself for speaking up and improving her lot in life. Suzie and Ryder aren't sure she's done herself any favors. "Where do you think he's taking her?" Ryder questions.

Mr. Rosenberg loads Mrs. Bing into the front of a blue pickup truck loaded with crates of oranges in the back bed. "Give me the little guy. I don't want him going where you are headed," he says, taking the child away.

"But I can't leave without my son," she cries.

The horrid Mr. Rosenberg takes the child and examines the boy. "He's rather cute. He looks healthy and of good form. My wife and I have a special place for this little boy." The wretched man stomps away from the truck with Sam, signaling to the driver to gun it. Before Mrs. Bing can protest her fate, she's whisked away down the dirt road. A thinner woman could easily have leaped out of the truck and fetched her child. Since she was destined to stay inside the vehicle, she sits silently in the passenger seat whimpering to herself. Had Rufus seen this, he would have been ashamed at her for giving up. Luckily, for the ethical crocodile, today he is swimming happily around Sanibel Island, completely ignorant of the constitution.

Ryder runs over to the man holding Sam. "Please, give him to me. I can take care of him while I work. I promise he won't slow me down," she says, thrusting out her arms. He may have been her brother for only a day, but the little guy didn't deserve whatever Mr. Rosenberg had in store for him.

"Listen, kid, all I've seen from your family so far is trouble. If you don't want any problems I suggest you shut your mouth and get to pickin'. If I don't see seventeen crates of oranges from you in an hour, you're going to regret it. Now don't worry any more about the baby. He's my son now. I haven't had an heir yet and with the way things are going around here, I won't. Six girls and not a single boy. That is pathetic. I should get a new wife and try for a boy with her. But until then, I will at least have this little guy," he says, lifting Sam up into the sunlight. What did you say his name was, again?"

"Sam," Mr. Bing says sadly, standing behind his daughters. He wants to fight for his son. He wants him back, but he also knows Sam is better off with the powerful Mr. Rosenberg than with him. If he stays a Bing, he's destined to pick oranges for the remainder of his life; if he becomes a Rosenberg, he can get an education, travel the world and be happy. "His name is Sam."

"I don't like Sam. Too short. I shall call him Samson. Come on, Samson, let's get you out of these old glad-rags and into something fit for a plantation owner's son. Ellen will be pleased to see you. She's your mom now. And you may have just saved her from being kicked out on the street for not giving me a son by now. Ten years of marriage and no heir. She should be ashamed!"

"So it looks like women don't have any rights in this new world, either," Ryder groans. "This is the worst week of my life! How can this be happening? Suzie, we have to figure out a way to stop this madness and get our old world back. The world where the sun always came up, the animals never disappeared, actions had appropriate consequences, bones stuck around and the constitution was the supreme law of the land."

Suzie nods in agreement. She looks toward the sky, examining the clouds, searching for one that looks like the cloud she wished upon in the first place. All the clouds look the same to her. They are white, fluffy and plentiful. "How do I know which one to wish upon?"

"Just do what you did last time?"

Mr. Bing doesn't know what his girls are doing and he doesn't care. He's worried about his wife and worried how he's going to pick enough oranges to cover the fact that Ryder and Suzie aren't picking and are instead staring at the clouds. He finds a tall ladder, climbs into a tree and begins picking oranges from the branches. His hands ache in three minutes, his neck burns in five and his back bends in ten.

Meanwhile, Beulah Bing is growing more worried by the minute. The pickup truck passed the store miles ago. "Where are we going?" she asks the driver, hoping for a positive answer. The old skinny man with a straw hat and wiry glasses just grunts in her direction. "Do you speak? Sir, do you speak?"

He finally looks at her briefly before turning his attention back to the road. "I usta speak. Back when I had a wife and family. But too many years as a slave has taught me to keep quiet. Now I do what I'm told and don't ask questions. Questions get me in trouble. Do you want trouble, ma'am?"

"No, I don't want any trouble, but I demand to know where I'm goin'."

"What, you think you got rights or something?"

"I had them yesterday!"

"You're crazy, ain't ya?"

She decides to change the subject. It's obvious he's part of the population who don't remember that yesterday the nation relied on the constitution. "What happened to your wife?"

"Old Mr. Rosenberg sold her. She was a better cook than a picker so he got good money for her. I was real sad when it first happened. I miss her real bad. But I know she's got a better deal now, working for some family in the kitchen rather than picking oranges all day. I just wish I could see her every once in a while, you know."

The worn and battered man pulls the pickup truck before a barbed wire fence and climbs out to unlatch the gate. He crawls back in and drives down a long, dusty road. The land is full of animals: cattle, sheep, swine and goats. Mrs. Bing gulps. This doesn't look like a better deal than the orange farm. This looks worse. This smells worse. This is worse.

"What am I supposed to do here?" she asks. "There you go again with the questions." He pulls up toward an old farm house and stops the truck. The house is in more distress even than her current home.

"I don't want to live here," she says, eyeing the place. "It's terribly dirty, lopsided and falling down. Plus, I have a family. I can't live without my family!" she cries.

"You don't have a family no more. Now get out and let me get on my way before I get a whippin' for being late when I get back to the orchard." He leans forward over Mrs. Bing's massive belly and opens the passenger door. "Get," he says again, pointing outside. "I mean it, lady, I ain't gettin' in trouble for the likes of you."

She obeys the old man and waves goodbye. He doesn't even nod. He speeds down the long, dusty road without turning back. Standing in the middle of the pasture, Mrs. Bing looks around. A few women emerge in the distance, slowly walking toward her. These women are frail, skinny and their burned, tired skin looks like well-worn leather. They creep toward her with dead eyes and blank expressions. Again she wishes running was an option. With nowhere to go, she decides to strike up a conversation instead. "I'm Beulah Bing. What is this place?" "You've been put out to pasture." Says an old woman with scraggly black hair that reaches all the way down her back. Her coal-black eyes are cold and harsh. If there's a soul behind them, Beulah can't see it. "We care for the animals. It's a dirty job, but somebody's got to do it."

"But I don't know anything about farm animals," Mrs. Bing objects.

"It don't matter. We'll show you."

Looking out toward the acres full of big, smelly, gross animals, Mrs. Bing wishes she'd kept her mouth shut when the hostile slave driver spoke to her.

*****

Suzie fixates on one cloud in particular. It resembles a locomotive steam train if she concentrates hard. Finally, she raises her chubby fist in the air, shakes it and screams, "I love rules!"

She lowers her fist and waits for results. Nothing happens. The sky doesn't turn dark. A twister doesn't brew in the distance. Thunder doesn't answer her plea. The slaves keep on picking, the bosses keep on driving and the day keeps on going.

"Well, Suzie," Ryder sighs, "I think it's time to pick some oranges."

Oranges

"**What's** for dinner?"

"Oranges?"

The Bing family, now short two members, sits on the living room floor, chewing on the oranges that weren't fit to sell. These are the oranges with yellowed rinds, tart middles and bug infestations.

Every muscle in their bodies ache. They are sunburned, exhausted, cranky and mad.

"Let's stage a coup," Suzie suggests, tossing a rind on the floor for the cats to play with. Tuffy, the cat, is on it like a chicken on a June bug. The cross eyed Siamese cat paws the thick peel with interest. This day is much better for him than yesterday, but he's still too shocked to speak about it. Then again, he's never spoken about anything before.

"We can't. We don't have the manpower, weapons or a plan," Ryder explains.

Mr. Bing doesn't speak. He misses Sam. He misses his wife and he misses his freedom. Suzie studies her father. She's never seen him like this before. He isn't the same. She feels terrible. A few days ago she had everything in the world and didn't even realize it. Rather than being grateful for her life, she was angry because they couldn't afford a present for Taylor's party. Now, Taylor's party seems a silly thing to care about. It's the last thing worth worrying over now. Who cares if Taylor is rich and decides which kids are cool in junior high? Being cool isn't everything. In fact, it doesn't matter at all in the scope of life's recent events. Suzie is happy to admit how important the rules are now. Rules govern all of life from the solar system to the tiny particles in the human body. With the sad expression planted all over Mr. Bing's face, Suzie wishes she could turn back time and undo everything that has happened. She can't bear the responsibility of having caused her family to become slaves to the awful Mr. Rosenberg. Getting her mother and Sam back are the first points of order on her to-do list. Somehow, she will stop the madness currently happening in the world. Things need to go back to the way they were.

*****

The sadness expressed in Mrs. Bing's eyes looks much like her husband's; only, her children aren't there to see it and for that she is grateful. As much as she misses them, she is thankful they are home. The obese woman sits at a long picnic table staring at the slop set before her. An old Indian woman with gray braids down her back tells her to eat before her supper gets cold. Mrs. Bing barely hears her. She's too busy missing her family and rubbing her aching muscles to care much about eating.

Her day was spent on the farm tending animals. It was a disgustingly dirty job and she hated every minute. Piles of poo littered the ground everywhere and trying to avoid the smelly piles was impossible. After several hours of carefully watching where she stepped, she finally gave up and began trudging through the messy mounds absentmindedly. Now, she's dirty, exhausted and smells like the animals herself. She desperately wants to shower and find a bed. Unfortunately, her housemates have different plans for her.

They expect her to wash the dishes since they cooked, changed the sheets on the beds and scrubbed the floors from where she tracked in cow poo. Arguing would get her nowhere so she wipes a sad tear from her eye, then carries her bowl full of squirrel stew to the sink, pours it down the drain and begins scrubbing the pots. Mrs. Bing has never been fond of cleaning, which is obvious from the messiness in her own home, nevertheless, she keeps working. There are no options. She has no freedom. As a slave, the rules are simple: do what you are told, stay quiet and abandon all hope. With every plate, her hope dwindles.

Off

Ryder opens her eyes. It's still dark outside, but she's freezing. Her quilt isn't heavy enough to protect her from the sudden cold spell. She sits up in bed and looks across the room at her sleeping sister. The clock reads 4:24. Luckily, her day won't begin for another hour and a half. Even slaves are allowed a few hours of rest before the daunting day begins anew.

Ryder creeps to the window, shivering with every step. This is unusual for Florida weather, but what hasn't been unusual this week? She fears with the chill in the air, the sun has died again. Peeling back the curtain, she looks outside and is amazed to see a massive blizzard raging outside. Piles of snow lay thickly on the ground like a dense white carpet. The wind howls. Ice clings to the bare tree branches like silvery hands. Gone are the orange trees. They've simply disappeared as quickly as they arrived. It's anyone's guess what lay in store for the world today.

Suzie's voice whispers across the dark room. "What are you doing? Is it just me or are you freezing, too?"

"No, it's not just you. We're in for another weird day. There's a blizzard outside. I bet the snow is three feet deep already."

"Are the orange trees dead?"

"Nope, they're gone completely. The orchards are gone. The owner's mansion is gone. It's like it never existed in the first place."

"That's a relief?"

A tiny cry echoes down the hall. "Sam?" the girls question in unison.

They rush to their parents' room and find Sam curled up in a little ball in his cradle, shivering. Mr. and Mrs. Bing hear his little wail and rush to his side. Mrs. Bing is so thrilled to be back home with her family that she doesn't even notice the chill. Then again, the extra three hundred and fifty pounds of blubber help keep her warm. The family embraces happily. It's a joyous moment. Not only are they reunited, they aren't slaves anymore. The terrible ordeal is over—at least that terrible ordeal.

"There's a snowstorm," Ryder explains. "We need to get all the blankets together that we can find and light the wood-burning stove. Whatever you can think of to keep warm, get it."

"It's snowing?" Mr. Bing says with true shock. "This has been one strange week, but I never thought it would snow here in May!"

"Daddy, go chop some wood for the fireplace. Mama, you go gather up the blankets. Suzie, for once The Weather Channel will be useful. See what they have to say. I'll take care of Sam," Ryder explains, forming a plan for the family.

No one gripes about their tasks. After a day of picking fruit, tending animals and being quiet, no one minds the little extra work caused by the strange weather.

From the big TV, a news reporter explains the new crisis around the globe. "As many of you have probably noticed by the sudden temperature swing, we are experiencing a gravitational shift on the Earth's axis. The long-term effects of this switch are grave. Meanwhile, in the short term we're left to deal with this massive change in climate. The icebergs are melting, causing catastrophic flooding, the desert areas are experiencing rapid downpours, it's snowing practically everywhere in the United States and we have no idea when the storms will stop. Obviously, this will have dramatic results on the environment. We can expect, if this continues, a massive extinction of most regional flora and fauna."

Suzie turns off the news, scoots Snicker, Feather and Gus off the sofa and sits down with her head in her lap, waiting for her dad to bring in the wood for the stove. There's no reasonable explanation why she should feel guilty about what is happening to the world, yet she does. She has this unexplainable feeling that her words to the sky on Sunday changed not only her life and the lives of her family members, but the lives of everyone on Earth.

With her parents busy at their tasks, she turns to Ryder for advice. "How I can fix this?"

"I don't know that anyone can fix this. It's just something we have to go through. Suzie, you're only thirteen. This isn't your fault. People say things all the time and it doesn't make the world go crazy."

"I can't say why I changed the course of events, but I did and now I have to fix it. Repeating a different phrase to the sky hasn't changed a thing. Every morning we awaken to a new set of oddities. And besides, I'm the only one who lost my bones. That proves this is about me."

Ryder pauses to think for a moment. Sam is nestled under a thick blanket in her arms, sleeping peacefully again. "We need to figure out what things we can make wishes on. Like, I know if you wish on a shooting star, your wish is supposed to come true."

"Yeah, and if you wish into a fountain," Suzie adds.

"Speaking of that, I once heard a story about a girl who wished into a fountain for summer to never end and it didn't."

"What happened?"

"I don't remember. I heard the story a long time ago. Anyway, you can make a wish on a birthday cake candle."

"What else? My birthday isn't for months."

"Let's look it up online and see what we can find." The girls sit down at the old 1980s–style desktop computer in the dining room and begin their search. They realize there are more wishing options than they realized. Not only can you wish on a shooting star and birthday candles, you can wish on a white horse, wishbones, ladybugs and dandelions. They read about their options. If you see a white horse, make your wish before you see its tail. When you finish your meal and have a wishbone left, each person should grab a side of the bone and pull until the bone breaks in two, then the person with the larger half gets to make the wish. When a ladybug lands on you, say, "Ladybug, ladybug, fly away home." Make a wish if it does.

To make a wish on a dandelion, find one with only the light, fluffy seeds left. Pull the weed out and blow as hard as you can, and if all the seeds fly away, make your wish. If seed pods are still left on the dandelion, abandon the weed and try again with a new flower.

"Which one should we start with?" Suzie asks.

"Well, we don't have the opportunity to worry about wishing on a white horse because there aren't any horses around here. And to be honest, with the horrible weather we're having, I doubt we'll find any ladybugs or dandelions around, either. Our only hope is the wishbone and we don't have any chicken in the fridge."

"Mom can get us some at the store later," Suzie adds, feeling hopeful.

"I don't think that's going to happen. There's no way, Camilla, our old rusty Buick, is going anywhere in this snow."

"We can't be out of options already. Keep looking. There has to be something we can wish on."

Ryder keeps researching and finally finds something she and Suzie have plenty of—eyelashes. "This article says that you can make a wish on an eyelash if one falls out. But you can't pull it out or the wish is null and void."

Suzie leans into Ryder's face, looking for a stray lash on her slender face. No luck. "Nothing. All your lashes are intact. Anything on my face?"

Mrs. Bing walks through the dining room carrying an armful of blankets. She isn't happy to see her girls sitting in front of the computer playing a game. "Girls! What are you doin'? We're in the middle of a blizzard and you two are just playing around. Do you take nothin' serious?"

"Mama, it's not what you think," Ryder tries to explain. She doesn't have the opportunity. In mid-sentence, the lights go off, the computer screen goes dark and the heater quits. Sam begins crying again. "What happened?" Ryder wonders aloud.

Mr. Bing steps through the front door, covered in snow and ice. He stomps his boots on the front step to shake off the powdery snow before shutting the door. The howling wind makes it almost impossible for him to get it closed and latched shut. Finally, he shivers and sinks down into the sofa, dropping a pile of logs on the carpet beneath him. "It's no wonder the electric is out again. The ice on the electric poles is thick. Looks like we're out of luck again!"

Ryder rushes over to her father's logs in the dark, anxious to get a fire started in the stove to warm the house.

In only a few minutes without heat, it's already getting cold again. Suzie digs through the drawers in the kitchen, looking for candles and matches. They completely forget about the eyelash theory even though there's one stuck to Suzie's nose as she hunts for candles.

A Wish

The light from the burning stove softly illuminates the messy living room in a dark yellow haze. Mr. Bing's small portable radio continues to update the family on the curious weather situation throughout the world. Birds are frantically migrating, bears are searching for dens to hibernate in and whales are trying to outswim the melting glaciers engulfing the Artic in floods of epic proportions. It's a nightmarish day for all Earth's creatures.

Expert scientists are back on talk-show panels, giving their opinions on how to fix the drastic climate change. Despite many theories and hopeful plans, nothing is being done to eradicate the problem. Perhaps nothing can be done. Is this the end? Has the world suffered strange oddities all week long simply to die off because of bad weather? Ryder doesn't think the future is as bleak as the experts' project. She still has hope. Hope in her sister. Hope that somehow Suzie can turn back the hands of time and save them all from extinction.

Ryder pats Suzie on the hand, startling her back to reality from a sequence of strange thoughts about white horses and dandelions. "I know you aren't going to like what I'm about to say, but I fear we have no choice."

Suzie stares at her sister's green eyes, wishing for once something in life was easy. She is sure whatever Ryder is about to propose won't make her happy; nevertheless, she is interested. Sitting in a cold, dark room swarming with chilly cats and a crying infant brother isn't her idea of a good time, anyway. "Tell me what you have in mind."

"There still might be dandelions or ladybugs outside. I know it's cold and everything is covered in thick snow, but if we go back to the lake and dig deep, we might be able to find something to help us make the wish we need to make."

"Really, Ryder?" Suzie groans. "That's your brilliant plan? I thought you were the smart sister. If we need something to wish upon, let's shoot for our eyelashes instead. They are right here and readily available."

"I know, but we can't pull them out or the wish won't work. They are useless to us."

Suzie leans in, studying Ryder's short eyelashes. For having nice, long hair, her eyelashes are rather stubby and sparse. Even if one were to fall out, it likely wouldn't have the power of a normal eyelash anyway. "There's got to be a loophole. I don't think it matters how the eyelash falls out as long as we don't pull it out. What if I rub my eyes until one falls out, then you make the wish on it?"

Unfortunately, by now, the eyelash once clinging to Suzie's pug nose is long gone and despite countless eye-rubbing efforts, not a single lash falls.

Ryder can't take the meowing cats or Sam's screaming anymore. "I need to get out of this house, anyway. I'm willing to brave the cold—even alone. If I find a ladybug or a dandelion, I will bring it home and you can make the wish. Since you're the one who got us into this mess, you should be the one to get us out. Ryder stands up straight and stretches out her long, skinny legs before announcing to her parents that she needs some fresh air.

"You can't go out in this awful snowstorm, you'll freeze to death in ten minutes flat," Mrs. Bing says between soft coos to Sam.

"I have to get outside. I promise to hurry. You won't even know I'm gone. Really, don't worry. I can take care of myself."

Suzie rises from the sofa, too, although her squatty figure makes less of a statement of camaraderie to her sister than she hoped. "I'm going with her. Don't protest, parents," she asserts. "This is something we have to do and we're doing it. Come on, Ryder, let's go."

Shocked at their daughter's determination, the Bing parents sit by silently. The girls find every piece of warm clothing they have and layer themselves into a clothing cocoon. As soon as they step outside in the arctic air, they almost turn back. "It's too cold. The wind is literally burning my face!" Suzie hollers through the roaring blizzard.

"If we don't try this, who knows what tomorrow will bring," Ryder retorts, trying to keep calm despite her fear. They've never felt cold like this before. It instantly chills them to the core, even their bones shiver.

White snow blows around their heads, making their front yard look more like a snow globe scene than a Florida swamp. There's no way to identify familiar landmarks. They are lost in a sea of white mist. "Which way toward the lake?" Suzie asks, confused by their surroundings.

"Luckily, Ryder's watch has a compass. She pulls up the sleeves of her sweaters and coats, trying to locate the rubber watch clasped around her skinny wrist. Even with the raging storm, the compass works. "This way," she says, pointing north.

Trucking through the deep snow is hard work. It's even harder than walking though water. Every step is exhausting. With the snow already up to their knees, they fear the trek back will be even worse. The snow falls rapidly, covering their fresh prints almost immediately. It's nearly impossible to stay on course, but Ryder follows her compass and trudges along armed only with persistence.

At one point, Suzie stumbles and crashes into a rock covered with ice. She cries out in shock. Ryder extends a hand and lifts her off the ground. Thanks to her bulky layers, nothing is hurt. No scrapes, bruises, dents or bumps. They continue hiking through the forest, keeping their eyes peeled for any signs of dandelions or small spotted beetles.

Eventually, they reach the edge of the lake. By now, the lake is completely frozen over with a thick sheet of fresh ice. "Guess we should have brought our skates," Ryder jokes, trying to make light of a troubling situation. Only days ago, the lake was warm and inviting. Today, though, it's difficult to believe it's the same lake, the same forest, even the same planet.

"I hope Rufus made it home before the storm hit," Suzie says, worried for the crocodile's safety.

"I'm sure it's cold on Sanibel, too," Ryder comments, trying not to think of the effects this weather would have on a cold-blooded reptile.

Without saying another word, the girls drop to their knees and begin digging at the edge of the icy water for signs of life. The grass is dead beneath the snow, leaving them feeling hopeless, cold and exhausted. "What's the point to any of this, Ryder? We're doomed."

"We can't think that way. Negativity breeds negativity. We have to think positive thoughts and believe this will work. Nothing good happens when you expect the worst."

Although Ryder's words sound good, Suzie is less than convinced. To her, the situation at hand looks pretty dire. Just as she's ready to give up and trek home, Ryder hollers to her from a few feet away, "I've found something. I think I found what we're looking for."

Don't Blow It

Suzie blinks the snow from her thick, well-planted eyelashes and runs over to her sister's makeshift tunnel down to the ground below the powder. Peering into the hole, she's amazed to see a single dandelion shielded by a pile of thin tree limbs protecting the area overhead from the masses of snowflakes that would have surely crushed the weed. "You really found one. It's amazing!" Suzie bends forward to yank the weed right out of the ground, but Ryder stops her.

"No, Suzie, don't! If you pull it out right now, the wind will carry the seed pods far away and we'll never be able to make our wish."

"You're right. I never thought of that! You are the smart one; I take back all the mean things I said earlier."

"We're both smart, little sister," Ryder says, bringing her ever positive and always encouraging warmth to the cold situation. "We need to figure out a way to move the dandelion without the wind getting to it. What are our options?"

"That sounds like a good plan, but it seems easier to just make the wish from here. If we dust off the snow from the branches and dig the tunnel out a little farther, we'll have room to blow the seeds far and wide with the wind behind us. I don't see why we have to pick the dandelion just to make our wish."

"You're right, Suzie. See, I told you we are both smart. Start digging—carefully, though, we don't want the snow to cave in around us and break the stem."

Within minutes, the girls have the perfect altar for their dandelion. The area around it is bare. Suzie slowly lowers herself to the ground, anxious not to disturb the surrounding snow. "I want you to do it," she says.

"No, if we stand any chance of this wild idea working, it has to be you to make the wish. Do you know what you are going to wish for?"

"Absolutely. But I can't tell you, it's bad luck."

"Okay, get ready. Take a deep breath and blow as hard as you can. I don't mean to add more pressure to an already intense situation, but you need to blow all the seed pods off at once for the wish to work."

"I know. I can do it."

Suzie inhales deeply, crosses her stubby fingers and hopes for the best. She lets go of her breath, releasing the air from her lungs with as much force as she can muster. As she does, she makes her wish: *I wish for the rules to return.* The wind catches her breath and scatters the seed pods away.

Ryder jumps up and down with excitement. "You did it, Suzie, you really did it. I'm so proud of you!" She envelops her sister in a huge bear hug.

"Do you think it worked?" Suzie asks, disentangling herself from her sister's tight embrace. "It doesn't look like anything happened. It's still snowing and cold."

"I don't think wishes are granted immediately. We might have to wait awhile."

"How long?"

"I don't know. We'll have to wait and see what happens. Life is like that. You do things and wait to see if you did the right thing. Often, it takes a while to see if your efforts paid off."

"What if it doesn't work?"

"There you go again with negative thoughts. If it didn't work, we'll try again. We'll find a way to fix things."

Saturday

Saturday morning, Suzie is the first to rise from bed and examine the day. She looks out the window. The snow is gone, the sun is shining and the orange orchard hasn't returned, animals are running about—all looks safe and normal. Feeling for her bones, she counts the cats. Every cat is present, even Winnie. Her ear, however, still hasn't returned.

"Ryder, get up, I think it worked!" Suzie shouts as she runs from the room to find her parents. To her amazement, they are awake, sitting in bed, talking and feeding Sam his bottle. "The snow is gone! The snow is gone!" she shouts.

"We know," Mr. Bing says, patting the king-sized bed. "Join us." She piles into the big bed with her parents and kisses Sam good morning.

"Do you think the madness is over?"

"Oh, I hope it is!" Mrs. Bing says. "I can't stomach another weird day."

"Go turn on the big TV and find out what's happenin' in the world," Mr. Bing instructs.

Ryder is already positioned in front of the big screen listening to the news. The local morning station gives the weather report, which is perfectly normal for a day of May in Florida. Hot and humid. Then they follow with a traffic report, which looks normal. No one mentions the series of odd events from the last week. Desperate for more information, Ryder turns the channel. By now Mr. and Mrs. Bing have joined the girls in the living room and are awaiting the news of the next chaos.

Even the national channels aren't discussing the sudden shift in weather or the Earth returning to its axis. There's no mention of the sun dying, Suzie's bones disappearing, the animals vanishing, actions having strange consequences, or the constitution's reenactment.

"What in the world is going on? Why are they only talking about the high prices of avocados? Who cares about avocado prices after the week we've had?" Mr. Bing asks.

Suzie's tummy turns over. What if this last week was only to teach her a lesson? What if nothing really happened and she only imagined it? Ryder seems to read her mind. "We didn't imagine these things. They really happened."

"How can we prove it?" Mrs. Bing asks.

"We have Sam. He's proof that the last crazy week occurred," Ryder shouts.

"And my ear is still missing," Suzie adds excitedly.

"Get Ms. Vall on the phone. We need to remind people what happened this week. This may only be a symptom of a much larger problem. Two days ago, only half the population remembered the constitution. Maybe we're the only family smart enough to remember the week's strange events."

"I doubt that's it," Ryder says, thinking there must be smarter families than hers.

Mrs. Bing hands the ringing phone to her husband. Wandy Vall answers quickly, hoping for a juicy story to turn her internship into a bona fide career. "Ms. Vall, this here is Mr. Bing. You wanted to interview us earlier in the week about my daughter's medical condition—the one where her bones just went missin' overnight. Well, I think we need to talk about that story as well as remind people about the dead sun, absent constitution, missing animals…"

Wandy stops him mid-sentence. "I'm sorry, sir, I have no idea what you're talking about. You clearly have me mistaken for someone else," she says before slamming the phone down on her desk. She fluffs her long red hair and looks at the other intern sharing her cubicle. "Why do all the weirdos call me?"

"She hung up on me," Mr. Bing reports to his family. "She said we never met. Had no idea what I was talking 'bout."

Ryder hustles Suzie out of the room so she can talk to her privately. "I think the wish worked. It's over. The rules are back in play. No one even remembers everything that happened."

"Why wouldn't everyone remember, though?" Suzie asks, truly confused. What's the point of all this happening if no one remembers?"

The phone rings, interrupting her thought. Mrs. Bing hollers down the hall, "Suzie, it's for you. Taylor wants to know if you're coming to her party tomorrow."

Suzie is speechless.

Ryder frowns. "I thought her party was last Sunday?"

"It was. I even talked to her about it. She was mad because the sun dying ruined her party."

Ryder runs to the kitchen. "Where are you going?" Suzie shouts, running after her. "To check the calendar. Sure enough, the daily calendar on the kitchen counter explains the dilemma. The last week never happened. Taylor's birthday party is tomorrow.

"Hurry up and answer the phone," Mrs. Bing demands, tired of keeping Taylor on hold.

Suzie picks up the receiver attached to the long yellow cord. "Hi, Taylor. Yeah, I'll be there. See you tomorrow." She hangs up and looks at Ryder. "So about that homemade gift you mentioned, I'm interested." The girls laugh.

"So it looks like you learned your lesson after all."

"Yep, rules are really important. It doesn't matter if no one else in the world remembers what happened, I do and I won't forget. Thanks to the rules, our solar system works, my body works, we have good laws that keep us safe and protect our freedom, our cats are back and every action I take has a set pattern of consequences. I like rules now. No, actually, I love rules.

The End.

Lady Jenniviere's Thoughts

What an unpredictable saga! I never realized before how important the natural laws and rules are to daily life. This is a good lesson to remember when you hate doing your homework, hate practicing, hate "being good." I struggle with rules sometimes too, but after reading this, I've learned that we all have to follow a certain system that keeps life predictable and safe. We're allowed to think outside the box and certainly should, but we also ought to respect laws and order while we create, play, learn, interact and imagine. Some rules need changing and nothing should be considered an absolute without first considering why the rule or law is in place. If it's a bad rule, we should fight to fix it. If it's a good rule, we ought to embrace it. Just as the sun rises every morning, so should we rise to every occasion and give our best—always. Ryder was right again, a positive attitude always prevails over a negative one.

Until next time.
Keep reading,
Lady Jenniviere

From the Author

I write Lady Jenniviere's Quill to make a difference in how children read. I want my books to offer important messages, to invite imagination, to show a different view point, but most importantly I want these books to teach kids that life isn't always wrapped up in a neatly packaged happy ending. Sometimes the hero wins, sometime they fail and sometimes the monster turns out to be the hero. Life isn't black and white. I hope my books illustrate the beauty of the gray parts.

If you enjoyed this story and want more like it, sign up for Lady Jenniviere's VIP readers list at:

www.LadyJennivieresQuill.com